"I am not your type of woman!"

Davina spoke breathlessly. "I'm a working girl who has the responsibility of caring for a brother and sister. Their future is my prime concern and you would find me very dull company indeed."

Nick's eyes twinkled devilishly. "On the contrary, I find you most refreshing. You and I, my dear Davina, are going to have a very interesting friendship."

Davina's eyes widened. "But—"

"Wait. Don't tell me you have no interest in men or marriage," Nick said. "Life is for the living, my girl."

"But, Mr. Tabor," she murmured, "I don't even like you."

A little smile lifted at the corners of his mouth. "You're wasting your time if you think you're going to change my mind," Nick replied. "I never could resist a challenge."

Other titles by
KATRINA BRITT
IN HARLEQUIN ROMANCES

Other titles by
KATRINA BRITT
IN HARLEQUIN PRESENTS

Many of these titles are available at your local bookseller.

For a free catalogue listing all available Harlequin Romances,
send your name and address to:

HARLEQUIN READER SERVICE,
M.P.O. Box 707, Niagara Falls, N.Y. 14302
Canadian address: Stratford, Ontario, Canada N5A 6W2

Flowers for My Love

by

KATRINA BRITT

Harlequin Books

TORONTO • LONDON • NEW YORK • AMSTERDAM
SYDNEY • HAMBURG • PARIS • STOCKHOLM

Original hardcover edition published in 1979
by Mills & Boon Limited

ISBN 0-373-02343-X

Harlequin edition published July 1980

CHAPTER ONE

'LOOKING for the Romeo, Cheryl?'

Davina stepped back from the flower arrangement to gaze on it with a critical eye and her younger sister turned round from the window with a guilty start. Her fair face in a frame of feathery curls deepened in colour.

Cheryl Mawne was sixteen, blonde and pretty in a kittenish sort of way, a complete contrast to Davina who was brown-haired and slightly taller. Both girls were like flowers themselves in their smart lavender pink overalls with their names embroidered on the breast pockets.

Cheryl sighed. 'I wonder why he bothers to come here when there are bigger and grander flower shops in the town?' she mused. 'Do you think he comes to see us?'

Davina chuckled and stepped forward to tweak a flower in place.

'I'm sure he doesn't. An experienced man of the world usually looks a little higher than flower girls. I bet he likes his women to be sophisticated and worldly wise.'

'Would you go out with him if he asked you?'

'He won't, and he's much too old for a babe like you. He must be all of thirty.'

Cheryl came to lean back against the till. 'Don't you want to get married, Davina?'

Davina worked in silence for a few minutes. 'I

haven't had time to think about it, I'm much too busy making a success of the shop. Besides, there's plenty of time.'

'In the meantime the right man might come along. What then? You could lose him and that would be perfectly awful. Doesn't it worry you?'

Cheryl shuddered at the thought of it. But Davina worked on unperturbed. The slender pearl-tipped white hands fluttered among the flowers, coaxing them cleverly into an enchanting array. She looked at Davina's dark head bent over her task, the delicate line of her profile, her eyes hidden by the thick fringe of lashes. She looked prettier than ever like that among the flowers.

'You know,' said Cheryl thoughtfully, 'I can imagine you bending over a pram as you're bending over those flowers now. It isn't natural not to want a boy-friend and dream about marriage. I dream about it all the time—wondering what my husband will be like, whether he'll be dark-haired, or fair like me. Which men do you like, dark men or fair?'

Davina smiled. 'Dark men, of course. They're more dynamic.'

Someone strode into the shop as she spoke. His hair was fair and clustered close to his head in curls and waves. His eyes were a deep grey, a wide-shouldered man, well built yet without any superfluous fat.

Cheryl giggled and Davina turned as he addressed them. 'I would like two dozen yellow tulips and a dozen roses, please. I have a card to go with them.'

His voice was deep and cultured and the hand he

slipped inside his jacket was well groomed.

'Certainly, sir,' Davina replied, giving a nod and a smile to Cheryl to attend to him. 'I trust the others were satisfactory.'

He drew a wallet from the immaculate jacket and extracted a card.

'Thanks, they were.'

He gave her the card and their eyes locked. For several seconds Davina battled to lower her gaze and found it impossible. Her heart was beating twenty to the dozen as her fingers closed over his card.

For goodness' sake, she thought, it's not the first time I've served the man! I suppose it's all this talk about men. Was it possible that he had heard her say that she preferred dark men? So what? It was true. In any case, this man was hardly her type —much too disturbing and used to getting his own way.

He was one of the new breed who pushed their way to the top, ruthlessly removing everyone in their way. She detested the kind. But he was a customer.

'Thank you,' she murmured, and moved to put the card down on the glass-topped table they used for wrapping flowers.

'Just a moment.'

She looked up at the peremptory words. He was looking at the flower arrangement she had been working on.

'Did you do this?' he asked.

'Yes.'

'Very artistic. Would you do one for me?'

'Yes. You can have that one if you like it.'

'I'll take it.'

'Fine. Cheryl will attend to you.'

Cheryl had put the roses and tulips in their plastic wrappers and was tying bows of wide satin ribbon around the stems of each spray.

Davina said, 'I'll make a cuppa, Cheryl.'

She hurried out of the shop into a room at the back, the doorway of which was covered by a beaded curtain, and filled the electric kettle.

Her hands were shaking as she switched it on, and she dropped down into a chair. This was the result of getting up at four that morning to go to the market for the flowers. She had worked all morning on a cup of tea drunk in a hurry before rushing out to her little van.

Such enthusiasm was all right in the warm weather, but this morning it had been bitterly cold. She could hear Cheryl talking to their customer and the rustle of paper as the flower arrangement changed hands. The next moment there was the sound of the door opening and closing.

Cheryl came through the beaded curtain with heightened colour.

'He asked me to thank you for the flower arrangement. He's using it this evening at a dinner he's giving at his place.'

She put her head a little on one side to examine her sister's pale face.

'Are you all right? You look a bit pale.'

Davina nodded. 'Just tired, I guess. I could certainly do with a cup of tea.'

'Coming up,' Cheryl smiled, and reached for the teapot. 'I do appreciate you leaving me on my own with important customers. It helps a lot. I'm not a bit nervous ... that is, not as nervous as I would be with anyone breathing down my neck.'

'I'm not the bossy type and I know my own sister. You might not love it like I do, but you do your best, and no one can do more.'

Cheryl spooned tea into the warmed pot. 'I do like it, you know. Your enthusiasm is kind of infectious. It's interesting working with someone who's keen on their job.'

Davina drank her tea, but it did not banish the wobbly feeling in her stomach. Cheryl had gone to fetch their lunch from a delicatessen just around the corner and Davina relaxed for a few precious moments over the order books. It made pleasant reading, but somehow this morning Davina could not whip up enough enthusiasm for it. Was it because spring was just around the corner and that the shop was now on its feet after months of hard work and heart-searching about making the right decision?

Difficult to believe that twelve months ago they had been a happy, compact little family living on a smallholding in the country. Her father had run a prosperous business providing fruit vegetables and flowers for a thriving community.

Davina still shuddered upon recalling the accident that had resulted in the death of her parents. They had been returning early one morning from fetching produce from Covent Garden Market when their car had crashed into a party of young people driving drunkenly home from a late party. They had been killed instantly.

Davina had been left the eldest of the three, Cheryl, Darren and herself. Fortunately she had been one of the reasons why the market garden had been so successful. Her skill with flower arrangements had brought in customers from far and wide.

Even so, setting up a shop was a venture that gave her qualms as to the wisdom of leaving the market garden. But good assistants who worked hard were few and far between and a woman was not likely to receive the same loyalty as a man, so it had been decided to sell the smallholding to their chief assistant who had long wanted a place of his own.

Cheryl had been happy enough to go into the shop on leaving school, but it had been mostly for Darren, their eighteen-year-old brother, that Davina had made the move.

A good-looking boy with a shock of dark unruly hair, he had not been doing very well. Spoiled by an indulgent mother, he could not have cared less about going on to a university. He was not a bad boy, just spoiled, and Davina was determined to do something about it. In her opinion he was devoid of incentive to any ambition, so they had sold the house and established themselves in a roomy flat where Darren was given a room with access to a roof garden.

Davina had encouraged him to cultivate flowers and shrubs and instilled it into him that he was now on his own and it was up to him what he made of his life. There would be enough money to see him through university, so he had to make up his mind what he was going to do.

He did. He decided to become a doctor, which meant that Davina just had to make a success of the flower shop. Cheryl was in a world of her own dreaming romantic dreams and taking every date she had very much to heart. She was sweet and vulnerable. By contrast, Davina was radiant, vital and oblivious of her own enchanting face and figure. She was too immersed in the task of making the flower shop a success. It was doing well. She had her quota of good friends to make her life full and exciting.

At least that was how it had seemed until her encounter with the big blond man in the shop. Davina closed the order book with a sigh and went into the shop to pick up the tulips and roses the man had ordered. There was a card with each in his masculine confident scrawl.

On one was written, 'To Darling Kate. All my love, Nick.'

The other said, 'Love and kisses, Nick.'

Davina smiled wryly to herself as she picked them up. Was Kate his wife and the love and kisses one his mistress? Both bouquets were in the delivery van when Cheryl returned with the lunch from the delicatessen.

The moment she arrived back in the shop Davina saw that something was wrong.

'What is it?' she asked as Cheryl put down the lunch on to the table before her face crumpled up.

'It's Rex,' she cried. 'He passed me in his car just now with a beautiful blonde. He was so interested in her he didn't even see me and they stopped close by to wait for the traffic lights. You should have seen the way he was looking at her, the beast! He never looked at me like that.'

Davina set the table and said matter-of-factly, 'I told you what kind of man he was—besides, you're much too young to be serious with anyone yet.'

Cheryl drew a hand childishly across tear-wet eyes. 'I wish I could be as hard as you are. Just wait until you fall in love! You'll have more sympathy for others then.'

'But I have lots of sympathy for you, dear,' Davina assured her gently. 'At the moment my stomach is crying out for food. Do let's eat.'

Cheryl eyed her balefully. 'Nobody's stopping you. Go on, eat! You can have my share as well. I couldn't eat a thing—I'd choke!'

'Nonsense.' Davina bit hard on her lip, wishing that there was someone who could help her in an awkward situation which seemed to be beyond her own powers to deal with. She decided to be diplomatic.

'You'll lose your looks if you don't eat a balanced diet. Who wants to go around looking yellow and dried up? Rex or any other man won't look at you then. Come on, sit down, there's a pet.' Her smile was beautiful. 'Tell you what, why not do me a good turn this afternoon by delivering the orders? Who knows, you might bump into some smashing hunk of man at Belcourt Mansions. The place reeks of money.'

But Cheryl was only half mollified and did not budge.

Davina tried again. 'Forget about Rex and I'll take you out this evening. I have a flower arrangement to make for a party at Belcourt Mansions, and I promised to take it round this evening. I was also invited to stay and join in the party if I wanted.'

Cheryl sat down at the table unconsciously. Her blue eyes were fixed in surprise on her sister's face.

'You gave that flower arrangement to Nick just now, didn't you?'

'Nick?' Davina echoed. 'Are you on first name terms already?'

Cheryl laughed and wiped her nose. 'I don't know his other name, do I?'

'Probably a double-barrelled one. Yes, I gave it to your Nick—and don't try to make anything out of it. It's business. You know we have to make as much profit as we can if we're to provide for Darren and you in the future. I can always take care of myself. Now let's eat.'

When Cheryl had gone to deliver the orders that afternoon Davina worked on the flower arrangement between serving customers in the shop. She closed her mind to thoughts of Nick deliberately, but found him creeping in subtly and equally determinedly to confuse her.

No man had ever affected her in this way before, much less a blond man. Davina had always pictured the love of her life to be someone dark and dynamic and dashing. Somehow she had never had much time for fair men; they were much too insipid. But one could not say that Nick was anywhere near to being insipid in appearance or in manner. He was too much man, one felt that instinctively. He was almost frightening. Davina, my girl, she told herself darkly, you'll have to go out more before you begin to shy away from men altogether. You know you want to marry just like any other normal girl, and if you're clever enough you can make the shop pay and land a husband into the bargain.

*

'The way to be really attractive is to use make-up sparingly. It has to be subtle enough to look natural, thus enhancing your looks instead of detracting from them. There, Cheryl. The blue of your eyes is echoed and intensified by the eggshell blue on your eyelids.'

Cheryl nodded and surveyed her pretty face reflected in the mirror.

'I see what you mean,' she agreed. 'Your eyes look as clear and sparkling as green rock pools, the way you've discreetly made them up. And there I've been shovelling make-up on.' She sighed. 'I'll never be as sophisticated as you, though. It's something you're born with.'

'Don't be silly. Sophistication doesn't mean a thing. You know what counts every time? It's sincerity which bubbles from a genuine warm nature. You have it, my pet. Like me, you love people and it shows.'

Cheryl giggled. 'You're beginning to sound like Mother. I'll always be grateful to her and Daddy for loving us so much.' She sighed, adding soberly, 'They were grand people.'

Davina nodded with misty eyes. 'And we mustn't let them down. We're going to enjoy ourselves tonight. No quaking!'

All the same Davina's heart was beating unevenly that evening when they entered the opulent flat at Belcourt Mansions.

Juleen Tabor was a well-known writer and broadcaster. She had made it to the top via crime novels, plays and film scripts. She was tall and soignée, a blonde who looked younger than her forty-odd years. The innumerable cigarettes she smoked not only kept her slim but they had given her voice a certain sexy huskiness that she used to full advantage.

Davina liked her because she was a genuine person who had come into her shop several times to place an order for flowers. She had been living in Paris but had come to London to publicise her latest book.

She bore down on them with a delighted chuckle on seeing the delightful flower arrangement in Davina's hands.

'Marvellous!' she cooed. 'And such good timing. The guests haven't arrived yet. Here's the buffet table. I see you've brought your sister. You must both stay—I like to decorate my parties with pretty girls.'

Chatting on, she took the flower arrangement and placed it in the centre of the buffet table.

'There,' she exclaimed with immense satisfaction, stepping back to survey the effect. 'Beautiful, isn't it? You really are clever, Davina. I ...'

Juleen broke off as someone strode into the room. Nick, thought Davina weakly, was even more devastating in evening dress with his closely cropped curly hair catching the light of the cut glass chandelier overhead. The jacket of his suit was beautifully cut to fit to perfection the wide, square shoulders. His eyes beneath fair brows were rapier-sharp.

In the shop that afternoon they had appeared to be grey. Now they were much darker.

He said forcefully, 'Where the devil have you been? Have you just arrived? I've been trying to get you on the telephone. I happen to be giving a party myself this evening. Why didn't you say you were giving one? Really, Juleen!'

Davina caught Cheryl's arm. 'Let's find the cloak-room,' she whispered urgently.

They were at the door when Juleen said, 'Don't go, girls. This larger-than-life man is my brother-in-law, Nick Tabor.'

'We've already met,' he said crisply. 'What about this party? I wish you'd let me know once in a while what you plan to do.' Thrusting his hands into his pockets, he ranted on, 'It puts me in such a damned awkward position!'

Outside the room Cheryl said with shining eyes, 'Isn't he marvellous? I'd love to run my fingers through those curls.'

'Marvellous?' Davina echoed the words in disgust. She looked at her sister in utter surprise. 'I think the man is downright rude. He didn't even acknowledge us.'

Cheryl laughed. 'He was too mad. I think he's a pet and I'm glad we have one friend here tonight. That looks like the cloakroom over there.'

They were discarding their wraps when the guests began to arrive. They were a motley crowd, most of whom were very well dressed. Davina noticed several celebrities when they entered the main salon and decided that the evening was going to be interesting.

A waiter bore down upon them with a tray filled with drinks and they were immediately surrounded by eager males jostling each other for their favours.

Davina saw her sister's flushed face and smiled with relief. It really was funny, after all. Cheryl had left a broken heart behind her in the flower shop that afternoon, and now she was being fought over—too ridiculous for words!

'Come, I want to talk to you.'

Nick Tabor had taken her arm and was bearing her away before she realised what was happening. By sheer luck she kept her drink steady as he ushered her into Juleen's writing room with book-lined walls and a typewriter on a desk.

'Now let me look at you. First of all I couldn't see you for flowers, now it's people.' He grinned whitely and pushed her down gently into a comfortable chair, then perched near to her on the corner of the desk. 'You know what I'd like to do at this minute?' he went on, leaning forward to bring his face tantalisingly near her own. 'I'd like to carry you off to some lonely wood and ravish you. How dare you look so delicious?'

Davina felt her face burn with embarrassment. 'Do you say this to all the girls you meet, or have you been drinking?' she gasped.

His eyes darkened with devilment. 'No to both questions. Finish your drink, then we can talk.'

With the feeling that she had never needed anything more Davina drank and emptied her glass.

'Sherry, was it? Like another?'

She shook her head, although the need for further stimulant was great. One needed something stronger than sherry when meeting Nick Tabor.

He took his time looking her over as he took the empty glass from her trembling hand, the slender figure in the wide-skirted dress, the brown hair curling slightly about her small head, her eyes very green as they gazed up at him.

As he watched her he saw the lovely eyes with

their slight upward tilt widen, then deep pink stain her cheeks. She cast him a wrathful glance and his well cut mouth curved in amusement.

'First the flower shop. Is it yours?' he asked lazily.

'Yes, it is—although I can't see what business it is of yours. And I don't know why you've brought me here. I'm not in the least interested in you except as a customer at the shop.'

He chuckled. 'What a mercenary little thing you are,' he mocked.

'And you're a wolf if ever I saw one,' she snapped back.

'But a nice wolf, wouldn't you say?'

'No, I would not. And now, if you don't mind, I'll go to see if my sister is having the same trouble.'

'You can't go at the moment when our conversation is becoming interesting.'

He bent towards her, and suddenly she was conscious of the frightening strength of his personality. It was easy to see that he was capable of being utterly ruthless when he had a mind to.

Breathing quickly, she said, 'Mr Tabor, I don't know why you've sought me out, but I can assure you that the feeling is not mutual. I'm a working girl who couldn't really interest you in any way. I have the responsibility of caring for a brother and sister who are without parents. Their future is my prime concern and you would find me very dull company indeed.'

His eyes twinkled devilishly. 'On the contrary, I find you most refreshing. You and I, my dear Davina, are going to have a very interesting friendship.'

Davina's eyes widened. 'But——'

'Wait. Don't tell me that you have no interest in men or marriage. Not with a very kissable mouth such as the one I'm gazing on now. If you have heavy responsibilities then a little light entertainment with a man in tow is just what you need.'

Davina had listened to him, every scrap of colour draining from her face, though her eyes never left his.

'Well, what about it?' he demanded. 'Aren't I right? Don't you think you've shut yourself away long enough? You can have all the flowers you want when you're six feet under. Life is for living, my girl.'

'But, Mr Tabor,' she said breathlessly, 'I've told you I'm not your type of woman. You'd be bored with me in five minutes of our meeting. I . . . I don't even know . . . what I think about you at the moment. I don't even like you.'

Despite the break in her voice she looked right at him. He returned her regard unwaveringly, a little smile lifting the corners of his mouth as he appeared to be smiling at some secret thought.

'You're wasting your time if you think you're going to change my mind. I never could resist a challenge,' he said, shrugging those wide shoulders.

The colour came and went in Davina's cheeks. Her clear eyes, a beautiful green, stared at him in horror. A small shiver ran down her spine. She was really frightened of the power he had to stir up some hidden chemical reaction to his nearness.

'If you won't believe me, I can't make you,' she told him with a quiet and, to him, unexpected dignity that did not fit in with the stricken look on her face. 'Only I can't see you making much headway with me against my wishes. I'm pretty strong-willed myself and once I've made a decision it stands.'

'I'm afraid it isn't your decision that matters,' he said inexorably. 'As I've already told you, I've made up my mind to educate you in the matter of men. They aren't all baddies, and I couldn't simply sit by and watch you hide away in your little corner taking care of your family and missing out on life yourself.'

Davina clenched her hands, hating him for speaking truths which she had consistently ignored—a life of her own, her own right to a husband and children.

He was smiling now. 'Perhaps I ought to qualify my last remarks a little. This notion you have of preferring dark men to their fairer counterpart is the real gist of the matter. I'm going to show you that colouring is not important. A man's a man for all that.'

His audacious grin rocked her frightened heart. He was a past master in the art of dealing with women, she thought angrily, only she was not just any woman. She longed to knock the grin off his face.

Looking back afterwards, Davina often wondered how she had managed to get through the rest of that evening. For years she had battled with an inner conflict that so often tortured her, namely the need to live her own life and the duty she owed to Cheryl and Darren.

She had suffered so much in trying to do the right thing for them and had never obtained much comfort from the thought that they would eventually find their own way in life without her aid.

Fortunately they had been blessed with wonderful parents who had loved and guided them in the right way through life—good grounding but vulnerable to the influence of the wrong kind. And young people were apt to be influenced by their companions.

Her heart beat unevenly as Nick Tabor stood up to tower above her.

He said, 'I have to go now. I called in to offer my help, but I have a party of my own pending.'

A feeling of relief gave her courage. He could not go quickly enough for her.

'So you did speak the truth about the flower arrangement being for use this evening?'

He coloured a little beneath his tan and his eyes narrowed.

'One thing you'll discover is that I'm not a liar. If I said that then it's true. Incidentally, I'm going to Paris quite soon, so I would like you to meet me one day for lunch before I go.'

'I'm sorry, but I shall be at work in my flower shop even sooner. I'm a working girl, Mr Tabor, so I would be obliged if you would seek your feminine company elsewhere.'

He was not in the least put out by the deliberate snub. Indeed it seemed to amuse him.

'The name is Nick, Davina. I seem to recall that you and your pretty little sister show your names on your overalls at the shop, so I'm telling you mine.'

'Thank you. I saw it on a card you sent to a lady named Kate,' she told him frigidly.

'Ah, Kate. Fortunately the lady doesn't need taming. Your second name doesn't happen to be Kate, does it?' he asked sardonically.

'No, it doesn't, and don't get any fancy ideas on that score,' she retorted scathingly. 'Regarding calling you by your first name, I really don't think it will be necessary since you and I will see very little of each other. Now if you will excuse me I'll join my sister.'

His hand came out to catch hold of her shoulder in a light but firm grip.

'It's no use, you know,' he said in clipped tones.

Davina frowned up at him. 'What do you mean?'

'That I mean to know you better and the sooner we start getting acquainted the sooner you'll begin to like me.'

'Like you?' she gasped. 'Why should I?'

'This is why,' he answered, taking her roughly into his arms.

It was like hovering on the brink of a fiery furnace, this agony of joy. The heat was there, rushing out and taking her breath away. She shrank with fear yet trembled with the exhilaration of ecstasy.

The next moment she was pushing him away with all her strength to allow her hand to come up and smack his face. Her own face burned like a fire, her eyes blazed.

'I don't think that's very funny,' she cried on a gulp of breath.

'It wasn't meant to be.' He stood tense and smiling a little. 'I've been longing to kiss you from the first time I saw you.'

Davina took a long breath, a long shivering sigh as if she had been shocked out of her senses.

'Could be that I've been wanting to slap your face

too since our first meeting. Your ego, Nick, is king-size. Now keep away from the shop. I don't want your sort for a customer. Slapping faces can become awfully wearing and I can't afford the energy. Goodnight!'

Davina fled from the room to look for Cheryl. For two pins she would drag her sister home with her, only it would be silly to do so when Nick Tabor was leaving.

Cheryl was talking to two young men in their early twenties who were obviously interested in her. As Davina joined her the guests began to drift into the buffet room. There was heaps of every kind of food.

The two young men used their long arms to procure plates for the four of them which they began to fill, and they munched contentedly. There was too much noise for anyone to talk confidently and Davina was too busy eating to look around for Nick.

She did not see him again that evening, but she could not forget him or his kiss. No man had ever kissed her like that before. It had been like an electric current running through her body and setting her quivering uncontrollably.

There was nothing to it, she told herself impatiently. The man was just experienced and it showed. But she had been kissed by men of experience before with none of the electric reaction that had fused her to Nick.

CHAPTER TWO

THE next few weeks were uneventful to Davina in the way that there was no Nick to brighten them. Strange how she missed him. Cheryl remarked on his absence several times.

'Did you know that Nick used to be in the Guards?' she said one day at a slack moment in the shop. 'That was before his father introduced him into banking. Now he's one of the leading international bankers.'

She had been gazing through the window. Now she was hugging her upper arms and gliding slowly around the shop as though dancing with the absent Nick.

Dreamily, she said, 'Can you imagine him with his uniform hat set on those fair curls, his legs in those long shiny boots and all that heavenly uniform?' She sighed. 'It makes you swoon just to think of it!'

Davina laughed. 'Life isn't like that, Cheryl, as you'll discover. Maybe you ought to have been a nurse or something like that. You wouldn't only have no time to dream, you'd see life as it really is.'

'It's an idea. How would I look in uniform? Some nurses today are wearing beautifully coloured overalls as pretty as ours.'

Davina said carefully, 'Who told you about Nick? You seem to know an awful lot about him.'

'I heard folks talking at the party Mrs Tabor

gave. He isn't married.'

Davina lifted her head from looking down at the order book.

'No? The man evidently believes in loving and leaving them. I bet he's had more love affairs than you or I have had hot dinners.'

'What if he has? A man of experience is always more exciting. Why don't you like him?'

'We don't know anything about him, do we? And that's bad. In any case I'm not interested one way or the other.'

Davina knew when she spoke the words that they were not true. She was continually thinking about Nick and wondering where he was.

A week later he strode into the shop as if he had never been away and her heart leapt in her breast.

Davina was alone in the shop, Cheryl having gone out to do some shopping for their evening meal at the flat.

For several palpitating moments Nick looked at her with unsmiling consideration, then sketched a faint bow which was supercilious in its lightness, and she felt her face grow hot.

'Good afternoon, Davina. I trust I find you well.'

'Very well indeed,' she replied. She knew her voice was crackling with dislike, but she did not care.

'That is indeed good news,' he said sardonically. 'It means you will be fit to go out with me this evening for dinner.'

She gave a slight start and he watched with pleasure the way her eyes with their tantalising tilt filled with a sparkling anger as she stared at him.

'Mr Tabor,' she said with a quiet dignity which

sat well upon her slender shoulders, 'I have no time for playing games. Is there anything you might be wanting—and I would remind you that I asked you not to come into my shop again.'

'Yes, there is something I want very badly. You,' he stated baldly.

'I'm sorry, but I'm not for sale, Mr Tabor.'

'It was Nick the other time we met. What's wrong in going out to dine with me? You'll enjoy it.'

'You mean you intend to. I shouldn't. I neither like nor trust you.'

'You don't know me well enough to either like or trust me. Why don't you find out? Or are you scared?'

Davina lifted her chin. 'I don't want to know you.'

'I'm perfectly respectable,' he said dryly. 'I have an elder brother who's a surgeon visiting the States, Juleen's husband. I began a career in the Guards because I loved horses, but my father wanted me to go in for banking. I gave it a trial to please him and found that it was not only exciting but that I had a bent for it. So here I am.'

Davina said coldly, 'I'm afraid I'm not as free as you, Mr Tabor.'

He lifted a hand. 'Nick, please.'

'Very well, Nick. I have a brother to see through his medical studies and a sister to keep on the straight and narrow. I work long hours at this shop and I have no time for love affairs.'

'But surely you have to eat. Surely you can have a meal out once in a while?'

'Not this evening, thank you.'

'Tomorrow, then?'

Davina pushed back a heavy wave of hair from her hot forehead. Today had been another heavy day beginning at half past four to reach Covent Garden for the flowers.

She shook her head, and the grey eyes narrowed on her pale face.

'Who does all the heavy work like delivering orders and fetching flowers from the market?' he demanded.

Normally Davina would have told him to mind his own business, but as usual his presence was turning her into a kind of zombie.

'We do it between us, Cheryl and I.'

'Then how is it that Cheryl is as bright as a button today?' He nodded at her look of surprise. 'Yes, I saw her just now on her way to the shops. While you're fagged out.'

She lifted tired shoulders. 'It's one of those days—and your appearance doesn't help.'

He said tersely, 'That's plain speaking anyway. Seems to me that you're doing all the donkey work. You're just a couple of kids playing at shop.'

'I'm twenty-four. At least we're earning a living.'

'And throwing your own life away in the bargain. Go and put your feet up in the back. I'll take over until Cheryl gets back.'

Davina looked at him as though he had gone mad. 'You must be joking!'

She stared at the beautifully cut City-going suit, at the imaculate silk shirt and sober tie. He looked like an advertisement for men's wear out of *Vogue* and he was proposing to sell flowers.

For answer he laid strong fingers on her shoulders, turned her round and marched her into the back of the shop through the beaded curtain.

The shop door opened as she sat down and she hoped it was Cheryl. It was two young women wanting bouquets to take to the hospital. Most of the flowers were marked with the price and Nick was soon wrapping up flowers that the girls were delighted with including the service, Davina thought wryly. The man could charm ducks off the water.

The shop door opened and closed several times after that, by which time Davina was fast asleep. The screaming sound of the electric kettle boiling awoke her out of what seemed to be a drugged sleep.

Opening her eyes, she saw Nick filling the teapot with boiling water. Looking at her wrist watch, she cried out in disbelief.

'It's five o'clock! Why didn't you waken me? Where's Cheryl?'

He put on the teapot lid and looked around for cups.

'Not back yet,' he replied lazily, and reached for the cups from a shelf.

'But she has to be. She went out at two to do a bit of shopping. I hope nothing has happened.'

'Drink this,' he said, 'and stop getting in a panic. She's probably stopped somewhere.'

Davina took the cup from him, her eyes dark pools of distress.

'She wouldn't stay out for three hours without telling me where she was going.'

'I said drink the tea.'

Warm strong fingers closed around her trembling ones and he lifted the cup to her lips. Davina gulped down the warm milky tea and looked up at him appealingly.

Far from feeling refreshed her head was as heavy as lead. Her tongue felt like sandpaper and her throat burned. 'I feel awfully ill,' she said. 'Please hold me.'

The next moment she had passed out. When she opened her eyes again Nick had put a cold wet compress on her forehead and he had his arms around her.

'Not to worry,' he murmured. 'I must get you home and send for the doctor.'

Thickly she said, 'I shall be all right. Our flat is here over the shop.'

He pushed a cushion under her head on the chair. 'Give me your keys. I'll carry you up when I've unlocked the door.

'I've telephoned for the doctor,' he told her, laying her gently on her bed. 'Do you think you can manage to undress yourself?'

She nodded, and he left the room. He came in when she was in bed. He sat on it to look at her gravely as he put the back of his hand against her flushed cheek.

'How's the throat? Painful?'

She nodded.

'I'm afraid it's tonsillitis,' he said gently. 'Cheryl has it too. She collapsed in town and is in hospital. They're keeping her in for a day or so.'

'You knew all along, didn't you, even before I awoke this afternoon, yet you didn't tell me.'

'What good would it have done? Had I told you you would have gone haring off to the hopsital and probably have collapsed there yourself.'

Davina was very aware of lying in a flimsy night-dress while he dwarfed the room with his size. She felt too ill and wretched to care much, but he still upset her.

'Is there anyone who can look after you?' he asked.

She thought quickly. 'My brother Darren is coming home tomorrow from medical school for the Easter holidays.'

He pushed the damp wads of hair from her hot forehead.

'Can he cook?'

'He'll be all right. He's very intelligent. I've tried to make him self-sufficient. Besides, if I have tonsillitis he can manage to make me hot drinks and cook a little for himself.'

The doctor came and Nick told him about Cheryl as he examined Davina.

'It's acute tonsillitis all right,' he said, placing a cool instrument on her tongue to enable him to peer down her inflamed throat. 'Keep warm, take hot drinks and the pills along with the medicine I shall prescribe and you'll soon be up again, young woman.'

Nick went out at the same time as the doctor to fetch the medicine the doctor had prescribed.

Nick stayed that night, giving her the medicine every two hours. Between doses she tried to sleep, but always something that felt like a web seemed to cover the back of her throat. Then Nick would hold her up in bed against his wide shoulder and give her a dose of some fiery burning liquid which seemed to burn a way down to her stomach.

She was conscious of him there, moving around or sitting quietly beside her, but it was too much of an effort to talk.

The next morning, with a light stubble around his chin, he made her a hot drink and sponged her hands and face. The doctor came again and Nick took him into the lounge while they talked.

When the doctor had gone Nick came in and sat on her bed.

'How are you feeling? The doctor is pleased with you and suggests getting a nurse in for a few days.'

Quickly, she said, 'I don't want a nurse. Darren is coming today. Thanks for all you've done. I couldn't possibly have managed without you. You can do one thing for me before you go—telephone the hospital to ask how Cheryl is.'

'I've already done so. She's much better and will be out in a day or so.'

Even after a night sitting up with her he still looked almost immaculate except for the golden stubble on his chin. She felt a vague resentment that he did not look in the least tired. The grey eyes still mocked and his mobile mouth still had that sardonic twist.

She looked down at her hands on the coverlet and spoke to them.

'Does Cheryl know I'm ill? I hope you didn't tell her I don't want her to come home and look after me when she's not well herself.'

'Cheryl doesn't know anything. She'll put it down to you being too busy with the shop to go and see her. About this brother of yours—you're sure he's coming?'

'Certain. Please don't stay any longer. You missed a night's rest and you need a shave. I'm awfully grateful, but we shall be able to manage.'

'You mean you can't wait to be rid of me?' The fair eyebrows lifted sardonically and she gave a pale smile.

'Don't take it personally. I just want to concentrate on getting better and I feel I can do that far quicker on my own.'

He reached for the hand nearest to him on the counterpane and curled his fingers round it.

'And you're not the teeniest bit sorry that I'm going?'

'Not really because ... you make me aware of what I'm missing ... how I would have lived had my parents been alive.'

'And you think that's bad?'

He was kissing her fingers one by one and she tried to free them to no avail.

Desperately, she said, 'It's a luxury I can't afford. Cheryl and Darren are at a crucial stage in their lives when they can either make or mar their future. I have to concentrate on them until they're firmly established in what they want to do.'

His eyes narrowed and the grip on her fingers made her wince inwardly.

'You mean you're off men until Cheryl and Darren are settled? Or is it that you're afraid of becoming too attached to some man ... me?'

She managed a smile. 'Let's say that you unsettle me and make me dissatisfied with the plans I've made.'

Nick's voice had been crisp and demanding. Now

some of the harshness was leaving his voice and Davina trembled inwardly. A Nick who demanded she could deal with, but a gentle charming Nick whose mouth curved upwards at the corners and whose eyes looked deeply into her own undermined her defences alarmingly.

'I understand,' he said gently. 'I'm glad I've managed to get through to you at all. You know what it means, don't you? You haven't yet become a hardened female who finds herself married to her career. I'm all for a woman being a woman.'

'You mean you don't like a career woman?'

He shrugged wide shoulders. 'Marriage is a career which I favour for all women. Granted there are some who don't fit in, but marriage and a career don't mix. A lot of women want their cake filled with the cream of both and it just doesn't work.'

Davina closed her eyes. She felt dreadfully weak in more ways than one. What frightened her most was the fact that as ill as she felt, this big disturbing man sitting beside her could still bring her alive to all kinds of needs she had been learning to suppress.

Weak tears oozed between her lashes as she recalled his gentle ministrations throughout the night. He had seemed to know the exact moment when her throat had been unbearably dry and painful, and she had drunk greedily from the cup he had held to her lips.

He had pretended to be half asleep on the occasions when she had felt the need to go to the bathroom. On her return he had swooped her up into his arms to carry her back to the bed.

'You've been very kind,' she whispered almost to herself. 'I shall be all right now, thanks to you.'

'Tears?' he mocked, bending over her to scoop them away with a long lean finger. 'I'll be going. I hope this brother of yours comes up to expectation, because he'll have me to deal with if he doesn't.'

Deliberately, he bent his head and kissed her quivering mouth, and her eyes shot open to gaze up at him darkly.

'Just to show you that I mean business,' he said with a smile that did not reach his eyes.

Davina drifted off to sleep and wakened to find herself alone. Feeling the need for a drink to ease her parched throat, she pushed herself up in bed and saw that Nick had left a jug of fresh iced lemon tea by her bed along with the next dose of her medicine.

There was also a large bowl of fruit on the bedside table. The large bunch of grapes placed on top of the pile looked inviting, but all Davina wanted to do was sleep.

When she wakened again it was well into the afternoon. Darren had not come and she began to wonder if anything had happened to him. Staggering to the bathroom, she splashed cool water on her face and put her wrists under the cold water tap to cool her down.

It was dreadful how weak she felt upon going back to bed. The day passed and the night too, a much better night than the previous one. Her throat felt better and she managed to wash herself in the bathroom. After cleaning her teeth and combing her hair she felt a little better.

The rest of the jug of lemon tea had gone during

the night, but she felt too fagged out to make more, unless ...

She made her way slowly to the fridge in the kitchen to discover another jug of lemon tea waiting for her.

Dear Nick, she thought. Thank you. Darren's bed had not been slept in. He evidently had not arrived. She heard the key in the lock an hour or so later. Her watch said nine o'clock.

'In here, Darren,' she called croakingly.

But it wasn't Darren who filled the doorway but Nick bearing a bouquet of roses and a scowl.

'So your precious brother hasn't arrived,' he barked, and placed the flowers on a chair before striding to the bed. 'How are you feeling this morning?'

She felt his cool fingers on her forehead, and her heart beat like a sledgehammer. It was difficult to define which was making her feel so lightheaded, Nick's nearness with his pleasing masculine fragrance of good grooming or her illness.

'I'm much better, thanks. I have no idea what's keeping Darren unless he's decided to spend his holiday with a friend, in which case he would be sure to let me know.'

He had found her sitting on the bed in her nightie in the act of picking up the telephone to enquire about Cheryl.

She felt his eyes upon her and was aware of the fragile nightie. Her wrap lay on the chair and she glanced towards it. For some reason she wanted that wrap desperately.

He said dryly, 'I suggest you get back into bed. There's nothing for you to worry about. I've con-

tacted the hospital and Cheryl is improving nicely.
I shall be calling to see her later.'

Davina was in bed before he had finished speaking. He looked into the jug of lemon tea, then at the medicine.

'I take it this is the second jug from the fridge. I'll make you some more. You must tell me what kind of books you like and I'll get them for you.'

Davina said weakly, 'How did you get in?'

Nick held up her key. 'I hung on to this.'

He turned abruptly at the sound of another key in the front door.

'Seems someone else has one too,' he added sardonically.

He strode out of the room to greet the newcomer and Davina heard his deep musical voice mingling with Darren's.

Darren came in the room looking rather sheepish and concerned.

'Sorry I didn't manage to come home yesterday, but we had a bit of a farewell party and I missed my train. How are you?'

Davina put out a hand which he took in his. 'I'm all right. Just a touch of tonsillitis. Cheryl has it too. She collapsed while out shopping and landed in hospital. Nice to see you, Darren. Sorry to land you with trouble on your holiday.'

He grinned. 'That's all right, I can study a patient at first hand. You must tell me what my bedside manner is like.' He came nearer and bent over her to whisper, 'Who's the man in the kitchen? Is he the doctor? He's just been telling me off about not arriving sooner—as if I knew you were ill. He made me feel about five years old.'

Davina smiled. 'He's a friend. Actually he comes to the shop for flowers.'

Darren frowned ferociously. 'You're not going to marry him, are you?' he demanded.

She shook her head. 'Of course not! He's been very kind to me, that's all.'

'Thank goodness for that.' He gave an immense sigh of relief. 'Sorry he isn't a doctor, though. I might have learned something from him.'

'You will,' Davina promised. 'He can turn his hand at anything.'

'He doesn't exactly look like a kitchen hand, does he? I'm famished. Anything in the fridge?'

'It's always pretty well stocked, as you know. Help yourself.'

Nick strode in at that instant with a tray on which stood a steaming bowl.

He addressed Darren briskly. 'I've made tea and there's a couple of slices of bread in the toaster in the kitchen.'

As Darren left the room Davina looked at him helplessly.

'I've never met anyone like you,' she said. 'You don't leave anyone a leg to stand on.'

He placed the tray down on a chair and came to the bed.

'If that's for me,' she said, 'I don't want it. I couldn't eat a thing.'

'You don't have to eat it. Just let it slide down your throat.'

He lifted her up in bed and placed the pillows behind her back. Then he placed the tray across her knees.

'I'll go to see how Darren is getting on with the

toast and I expect that bowl to be empty when I come back,' Nick told her darkly.

With the feeling that he was quite capable of feeding her if she did not eat Davina picked up the spoon.

CHAPTER THREE

In no time at all Davina and Cheryl were back in the shop again. Neither of them felt too fit, and it showed in their conversation. Cheryl had always been a bit of a dreamer; now she seemed to dream more than ever. It bothered Davina to see how she had withdrawn into her own little world.

Was she in love with Nick? He had gone to see her at the hospital and she had never told Davina what had passed between them. She was so young and Nick so very experienced.

Darren had been a brick in looking after them during his holiday. At least he was settled enough and did a fair amount of homework while he was at the flat.

During that first week back in the shop Davina found herself wishing that she could shake off the feeling of disturbance that was always with her since Nick had gone away. He had left for Brussels the day after Darren had arrived and had sent flowers every day. They had come to the flat fresh with the dew still on them and that had been the only time that Cheryl had mentioned him.

'Funny, isn't it, sending us flowers when we live among them? They must have cost him the earth. Did you see Rex when I told him they were from an admirer?'

Davina had shaken her head. 'I still think you're wrong to make it up again with Rex. He'll let you down again—he's that sort.'

But Cheryl had only laughed. 'Well,' she argued, 'he has the kind of money that takes us to the best places. By the way, his aunt in Kent has invited us down for the weekend. You will go with us, won't you?'

Davina stared at her sister in astonishment. 'Why in the world would you want me to go with you? I should only be in the way.'

'But you wouldn't. I think his aunt wants to see what kind of family I've got. Please say you'll come.'

'I'll think about it,' Davina promised.

It was only one of the things Davina had to think about. The trouble was one could not shut out memories as disturbing as those of Nick. The sign of any young man blond and wide-shouldered who faintly resembled him set her heart going nineteen to the dozen. It was so odd that one man could disturb the even tenor of her life, but there it was, and it was very frightening.

Each night Davina lay in bed staring into space, into emptiness. She saw something go, taking part of her with it and leaving nothing behind. Each day she was back in the shop where a man's half mocking eyes had captured her own, stirring an old fear in her mind. Disturbing grey eyes and a mouth that could be cruel and ruthless or soften into tender humour while he ordered flowers for one or two of his lady loves.

Before the weekend, on early closing day, Davina took Cheryl to town to buy new clothes, and ended up with replendishing her own wardrobe. The extravagance for Cheryl was justified because it was essential. For herself it was in retaliation for Nick's entry and exit from her life.

They went down to Kent directly after the shop closed on Saturday in Rex's big car. The spring weather had improved enormously and it was quite warm.

The house lay in acres of woodland and gardens, the latter glowing with all the beauty of an English spring; daffodils, crocus, narcissi, and violets. However, the house itself was Georgian and very homely with chintzes and lots of flowers.

Lila Stanford, a smart woman in her fifties, greeted them on their arrival. She and her husband George were celebrating the arrival of their first grandchild. These birthday celebrations marked a complete gathering of the family.

The eldest daughter Corinna, married to an Oxford don, had produced the first grandchild. There was a son the same age as Rex and a younger daughter still at boarding school.

Lila and Rex Martin's mother were sisters. His parents were still away on a winter cruise. Davina had never liked Rex Martin. In her opinion he had never grown up for all his twenty-five years. He was irresponsible and far too fond of a good time. Cheryl was not the girl for him. She was too vulnerable, too trusting and idealistic.

Rex dabbled in painting and had sold one or two pictures. But he existed mostly on large cheques provided by a doting mother. His parents owned property in the heart of London and he had a penthouse in one of their properties in Knightsbridge.

Lila Stanford greeted them charmingly. 'So happy to meet you,' she said warmly. 'I believe you've both been ill. I want you to regard this house as your home for this very brief visit, and do enjoy yourselves.'

To Rex, she said, 'Dave is looking for you. I've put you in with him. Do go and find him while I take the girls to their room.'

She escorted Davina and Cheryl upstairs, chatting on the way about her family whom she obviously adored.

'George, my husband, is overwhelmed about our grandchild and we shall be celebrating this evening with a dance and a party.'

Her look at the two girls was warmly appraising. Their spring suits were very becoming and this latest girl Rex had taken up was certainly different from the usual fast set he went around with.

She remained talking to them until someone called her from below.

'Please excuse me, won't you?' she asked, smiling apologetically. 'You'll soon find your way about. By the way, we have an indoor swimming pool. If you look through your window you'll see it—or rather the glass roof. We had it built on at the back of the house. You can stop in to look at the baby in the nursery on your way down if you wish. Come down when you're ready.'

When she had gone Davina and Cheryl smiled at each other.

Cheryl said, 'Glad you've come?'

Davina nodded. Her charming face softened. 'Let's get ready so we can peep at the baby.'

When, after inspecting the baby, they went down to the lounge Lila's husband George came forward to greet them.

'Sorry I wasn't here when you arrived,' he said, shaking hands warmly.

A dapper man well into his fifties, he was still slim and athletic. His brown hair, sprinkled with grey, was receding at the temples, but for all that he did not look his age.

'I'm on top of the world today,' he went on. 'Seen my grandson yet?'

Davina laughed. 'Yes, he's a poppet. How proud you must be.'

George introduced them to his family, Corinna who was small and brown-haired like her father, David who was dark and serious and Jane the youngest girl. George took Davina in to dinner and Cheryl went with Rex. Davina sat by David who was shy and very different from his cousin Rex who sat opposite to her with Cheryl looking charming in her evening dress of pale blue chiffon.

The dinner was very enjoyable, with everyone toasting the new baby in champagne. Presently, in the room cleared for dancing, Davina was claimed by several young men.

The dancing was in full swing when Davina paused between partners to look for Cheryl. Suddenly someone took her in his arms and she was swung into the next dance number. She was laughing up at him when the expression on her face became fixed.

'Nick!'

She cried his name in utter surprise as he smiled down at her. Davina was of medium height, not too tall or too small, yet she was well below that lean strong face from which grey eyes studied her intently. She would have been very uneasy had she been able to read his thoughts.

Nick Tabor was a connoisseur of beautiful women. He regarded them as essential to the background of everyday life. He had enjoyed taking them out to shows and meals and with a hint of cynicism he would admit that the affairs he had indulged in had been fun while they lasted.

As for settling down with one of them, such an idea had never been entertained for long. His work was the prime factor in his life and he worked as hard as he played. He wanted nothing changed. Yet since meeting this slip of a girl with her beautiful brown hair as shining and rich as any blonde, he had been immediately drawn to her.

Granted, had she fallen into his arms as the others had done he might have forgotten her, but since meeting her he had experienced a startling impulse to seize her in his arms and hold her close. But holding her thus was giving him no satisfaction. There was no clinging to him, no adoration in her lovely eyes. She danced as lightly as a leaf borne on the wind, and the lack of spontaneous surprise about her piqued his vanity.

Her untouched look of utter serenity piqued him too. It made him very aware of her in his arms, aware of the sudden quickening of his pulses. Never had he imagined that one day he would meet someone who would be different for him from all the other women he had known.

This girl he knew from experience was entirely unawakened, and while his intelligence demanded a woman who was not naïve in any way somehow it did not seem to matter. All he knew was that he had never expected to meet a girl who could make all the other women he had known unimportant. He was discovering that there was something, some chemical reaction inside him that responded to the unconscious appeal she made to his animal instincts. He wanted to have her yet treat her gently. She appealed to his better nature, yet she fired him with an urgent need to possess her.

He could never suffer fools gladly, neither could he stand simpering, shallow women no matter how beautiful they might be. This girl was neither. She had character and she was exciting. He had never faltered on being challenged, and Davina threw a challenge which made him feel alive and vibrant. What would be the outcome he neither knew nor cared. He only knew that from the moment their eyes had first met something had happened to him that was very beautiful and stimulating.

Davina came out of a sense of shock at seeing him again with a startled little gasp. The colour swept to her cheeks as a strange frightened feeling swept through her whole being.

'Where ... where did you spring from?' she gasped. 'I ... I never expected to find you here.'

He smiled and guided her from the dancers to the edge of the floor.

'Are you better?' he enquired politely.

'Yes, thanks. I'd like to thank you again for what you did. Cheryl is here too. We've been invited for the weekend.'

'I'm glad. So have I. There isn't much of you, is there? It's like dancing with a will-o'-the-wisp. Any minute now you're going to be borne upwards on a moonbeam to outer space leaving me dejected and alone.'

He laughed down audaciously into her face and her heart began to slip out of control.

She laughed. 'Too bad you'll be too big to follow me,' she teased, feeling absurdly happy and light-hearted.

He said darkly, 'Beware, I have long arms. What I possess I don't give up easily. How is Darren?'

'Fine. He's gone back to medical school. He's settling down nicely, I'm happy to say.'

'But he won't have anything nice to say of Nick Tabor?'

'He appreciated your kindness to me.'

He said dryly, 'That was very noble of him. You want someone at the back of you when dealing with teenagers. A woman is no good on her own.'

She was immediately on the defensive. 'I'm doing fine up to now. We're a very compact little family and are happy together providing no one disrupts us.'

'In other words you want to be left alone?' He digested this, then added coolly, 'And you're happy about Cheryl and Rex?'

Davina looked up at him sharply. 'What do you mean?'

'Simply that she deserves someone better. She needs looking after, and Rex delights in looking after number one—himself.'

The frankness of her regard disarmed him. 'But aren't all men selfish?'

He laughed. 'True. But don't tell anybody, will you? You'll spoil my fun.'

She said dryly, 'I doubt if anyone can do that. You'll have your own way regardless, I'm sure of that.'

Nick raised a provocative brow. 'True again. You seem to know me fairly well. It might interest you to know that I've been trying to make up my mind about you.'

Her fingers moved a little in his hold as he guided her away from boisterous dancers.

'Really? I should feel flattered, but I don't. It only means that you're at a loose end and therefore dangerous to naïve girls like myself.'

He swung her round and piloted her to the door.

'Now let's see if you're as brave when we're not in a crowd of people,' he murmured darkly.

Davina found herself in the garden before she realised what had happened and she shuddered suddenly in the night air. The weather had been warm for spring, but the nights still very chilly.

Nick had whipped off his jacket and was placing it around her shoulders. His breath was warm on her cheek as he bent his head to breathe in the fragrance of her hair.

His body heat retained in the jacket seeped into her very bones. It was almost as if his arms were around her.

It was both maddening and embarrassing that she could think of no cutting reply.

She found herself saying rather defiantly, 'It's rather chilly, as you'll discover now that you've shed your jacket. Please take it back. I'd hate to think that you might catch a chill through being so chivalrous.'

Her hand, already lifted, was taking the jacket from her shoulders, but his hand was on hers preventing her.

'I won't catch a chill,' he told her confidently. 'In

any case I shall have plenty of the stuff that cheers later this evening with George.'

Davina looked at him aghast. 'You mean you're going to sit up half the night drinking with him?'

He placed an arm loosely around her shoulders and walked her into the garden along one of the paths.

'Yes,' he replied. 'We're having an orgy when all nice little girls are in bed.'

She heard the laughter in his voice and looked up at him indignantly.

'I might have known you were having a joke at my expense! Although I wouldn't put it past you, having indulged in that kind of thing in the past.'

'You're determined to think the worst of me, aren't you? I wonder why? Is it because you're afraid of liking me too much?'

Davina stopped in her tracks. Some sixth sense was warning her to turn back to seek the safety of numbers inside the house.

'I think we'd better go back in, don't you?'

'So you *are* afraid of me.'

Nick placed one hand beneath the jacket at her back and the other crept slowly around her. He gave her a wry smile as his hand moved over her back.

'The only way to get over your fear of me is to get to know me better.'

He bent his head as he spoke and set his mouth lightly to hers. His kisses were light and friendly. But if they were meant to be that Davina's heart responded to them madly.

She melted against him as his kisses deepened. The blood ran hotly in her veins. Everything was forgotten in the joy of soaring as it were above all earthly things.

But she was too dedicated to her commitments and to her family to forget them for long. It was an effort to set her feet on the solid earth again, but she managed it.

'If that was to pay for the loan of your jacket then you've been amply rewarded. Here, take it.'

Slipping out of his jacket, Davina flung it at him and fled into the house. Lila came to her as she was standing to recover herself.

'Ah,' she cried, 'there you are. Have you seen my husband anywhere? I believe a friend of ours, Nick Tabor, has arrived and I thought George would be with him in his study, but he isn't there. You don't happen to have seen a tall, fair young man anywhere around?'

Davina felt her face grow hot. 'I didn't know you were friends of Nick Tabor.'

'My husband has known him for years and Corinna fell passionately in love with him before she met her husband. But then all the girls fall for Nick. Do you know him?'

'He's one of our customers at the shop,' Davina told her.

'Then you do know him. The trouble is he's always so hard to pin down for a party. He only came here this weekend to talk over some invest-ments with George. Nick has a mind and memory like a computer. If he worked for himself instead of being an international banker, he'd make a fortune.'

'How lucky for him,' Davina said dryly.

Lila lifted finely pencilled brows. 'Do I detect a note of censure?'

'Not really, but if there's anything I hate it's these so-called human computers.'

Even as she spoke Davina felt a presence behind her back. By the way her pulses were racing it could only be Nick.

'Why, Nick, we were just talking about you.' Lila's light laugh was beyond malice. 'I'm afraid Davina doesn't care for you very much.'

'Obviously she has poor taste in men—or should I say no taste at all for them,' he mocked from somewhere above her head. 'However, perhaps we can change her mind during her stay in your delightful house.'

Lila shook her head as though such problems were beyond her.

Playfully she said, 'Do you know, Nick, I have a feeling that George can't be far away now I've found you. You have some business with him, I believe.'

Nick gave a mocking half bow. 'That is so, madame,' he assured her teasingly. 'However, I hope I don't find him yet, because I haven't eaten since early this morning on the plane from Paris and I don't care to drink with him on an empty stomach. I have to keep my brain alert. It's what I'm paid for.'

'Oh, you poor thing! Why didn't you say? Come along, I'll see that you're fed. Excuse us, Davina.' Thrusting her arm through Nick's, Lila led him away, at the same time saying over her shoulder, 'Here comes David. I think he's looking for you, Davina.'

In bed that night Davina lay waiting for Cheryl to come. Although Nick had not put in an appearance again she felt his presence in the house as she felt it now at this moment. It was unsettling to say the least and every ounce of resistance she was capable of rose hotly inside her.

He was spoiling what otherwise would have been an enjoyable weekend. It came to her then in a blinding flash. She who had scorned the charms of blond men was hoist with her own petard. She was in love with a man whose type she had never really been interested in. If it was not so painful she could have laughed at the irony of it.

Shaken as she had never believed herself capable of being, Davina lay staring wide-eyed at the ceiling. She recalled his kisses and despised herself for her own response.

Cheryl came creeping in the room in the small hours.

'Have a nice time?' Davina asked as her sister undressed.

'So-so. I've had a beastly toothache on and off and I'm just about to go mad with it.'

Davina was out of bed immediately, pushing her feet into bedroom mules and scanning Cheryl's face anxiously.

'You poor dear,' she said sympathetically. 'I'll go and get you a warm drink. I have some tablets in my bag. Those should do the trick. Shan't be long.'

Davina was going carefully downstairs in order to make the least noise when she met Lila coming up. Quietly she explained the situation. Lila sympathised and directed her to the kitchen.

'The staff will have gone to bed, but I'm sure you

can cope. You'll find plenty of milk in the fridge.'

The light was on in the kitchen when Davina pushed open the door and the air was warmly scented with freshly made coffee.

'Come in, don't stand there,' invited Nick, lounging back in a chair which was balancing on its two back legs. He was demolishing a plate of sandwiches and a steaming cup of coffee.

Davina had never expected to meet anyone in the glaring lights of the kitchen, hence her fragile negligé. She stood poised in the doorway, aware of her figure leaving little to the imagination beneath the delicate covering.

She backed away. 'Sorry to disturb you. I'll come back later,' she told him.

The chair beneath him righted itself with a crash as he rose to his feet.

'For crying out loud!' he snapped. 'Tell me what you came for—or better still help yourself. I'm not pigging it. George got hold of me before I could eat.'

He leaned with the flat of his hand to steady himself on the kitchen table and glowered.

'And don't look at me as though I'd just crawled out from beneath the floor boards. Anyone who's fool enough to drink on an empty stomach usually ends up being slightly inebriated. So come in, my sweet, and let me be a lesson to you.'

With the thought of the suffering Cheryl in mind, Davina obeyed unwillingly.

She explained, 'I've come for a hot drink for Cheryl. She has a toothache.'

Nick lifted a hand. 'Say no more,' he said, and dropped back into his seat.

Never had milk taken so long to heat up, Davina thought, as she watched the pan on the stove. It did eventually and she washed the pan and returned it to its place.

Nick had resumed his eating and drinking, eyeing her with narrow-eyed appraisal.

'I wish you wouldn't stare at me so much,' she said. 'I find it very embarrassing.'

He said crisply, 'The next time you come down to the kitchen in the small hours put something more serviceable on, otherwise you'll be giving people ideas.'

She lifted a militant chin. 'And the next time you come down to the kitchen you might take the tray up to your room to eat it.'

He grinned. 'What, the tray?'

'You know what I mean!'

'Sorry,' he said. 'Stay and have a cup of coffee with me.'

'I don't think that would be wise in my present attire, do you?'

He laughed and stretched out his long legs contentedly.

'One of these days I'm going to take you in hand and show you what you're missing. You're much too serious for your age.' He eyed her darkly. 'I suppose I asked for that crack. Take care, you should never provoke any slightly inebriated man. It's asking for trouble.'

Davina eyed him resentfully. 'From where I'm standing you spell trouble in any case. Goodnight, Nick.'

He was on his feet and opening the kitchen door for her.

'It's good morning, my sweet,' he mocked. 'Tell Cheryl I'm sorry to hear about the toothache. Sleep well.'

But Davina did not sleep well that night. She awoke early not much after seven to find Cheryl still sleeping. The pill and hot milk appeared to have done the trick for her toothache.

Padding softly to the window, she looked down below to gaze on the glass roof of the indoor swimming pool. Smiling to herself, she put on one of her new brief swimsuits, threw on a wrap and picking up a towel slipped quietly out of the room.

She met no one on her way to the pool where she dropped her wrap and towel and dived in. The water was warm and it was heaven to glide under the surface along the length of it.

It had been some time since she had done any swimming and it was fun to climb up to the top of the diving board and practise diving. She stood for seconds on the diving board to adjust her bathing cap. Then she made a graceful arc in the air and hit the water in a perfect dive.

'Bravo!' said a musical drawling voice, and she swam to the side of the pool to see Nick sitting there in his trunks, grinning.

Davina could only stare back at him, the colour draining from her face. Once again the old familiar pounding of her heart evoked by his presence deafened her to everything else. Once again she felt the need to cover herself up against those keen intelligent grey eyes.

He had evidently been in the pool and had been watching her for some time.

'Hi,' she answered, and swam away from him.

She was more than half way along the length of the pool when he caught up.

'Practising for the Olympics?' he grinned. 'Why must you always run away? Are you playing hard to get in order to keep me interested?'

Davina did not bother to turn her head to show her disgust at his king-sized ego.

Swimming strongly, she said, 'Will you please go away. I was enjoying myself until you came.'

'I was already here when you arrived, have been for some time,' he answered, doing a slow powerful crawl beside her. 'How is Cheryl?'

She said shortly, 'Asleep when I came out, as I thought you would be. You certainly keep strange hours, Mr Tabor.'

He spoke savagely. 'The name is Nick—and there's nothing strange about me going to bed at dawn and rising later with the lark, as the saying goes.'

Something in his tone ought to have warned her. The next moment he had grabbed her in his arms and she found herself fighting him with all her strength. Fighting with him was exciting despite her anger. But she knew the outcome of it long before it ended. However she kicked and hit out at him it was impossible to evade the brute strength of his arms.

'Let me go, you big ape!' she cried, all to no avail.

At last, spent and quivering, she was clamped hard against his hard body. She saw the flash of white teeth, the grin of the victor as he bent his head and took his reward.

Gradually her whole body became limp and she stopped treading water. Her heart was beating wildly and time stood still as she clung. Deeper and deeper went Nick's kiss until Davina felt that he was taking away her very soul.

It came to an end suddenly when he stopped treading water too and they sank beneath the surface. The next moment she was free and making for the side of the pool. Within minutes she was picking up her wrap and towel and running off to the house.

CHAPTER FOUR

LOOKING back on that weekend Davina could not say that it had been a success. Upon returning to her room she had found Cheryl awake with raging toothache, and it had only been after much telephoning around that they managed to contact a dentist who consented to see her.

Rex had driven them the twenty miles to the dentist and the offending tooth had been removed Then it had rained after lunch on their return and pleasures were restricted. There were no outdoor activities like tennis or walking, and the house seemed to have lost its magic to Davina because Nick had gone.

He left while they were on their way to the dentist, so they did not see him again. To cap it all Cheryl and Rex had a blazing row, the cause of which she refused to divulge to Davina.

Rather bitterly, Davina blamed the change in Cheryl and herself on Nick. She knew it was unfair to do so, but there it was. He haunted every waking moment of her life and Cheryl, withdrawn and quiet, was another problem which she had not the slightest idea how to cope with.

They stayed in most nights in their flat after work. Davina usually concerned herself with the affairs of the shop while Cheryl amused herself playing records or reading.

Nothing much happened in the days which

followed until one day Rex swaggered into the shop.
Cheryl was at the hairdressers. Davina had been to
have her hair styled the previous day. The result
was a shining cap of brown silky hair falling in soft
natural waves around her face and giving it a kind
of piquancy that was very becoming.

Cheryl had been loud in her praises. 'It suits you,
Davina. You look beautiful. I must have mine
done. Do you think it will suit me?'

'Of course,' Davina had told her confidently.
'Like me, you have thick luxuriant hair, so you
won't get that boyish look with it shorter. Besides,
I'm sure a change is good. Sometimes we tend to
get into a rut, so why not be something different
from our usual boring selves? What about going to
the hairdressers tomorrow? I'm sure they'll fit you
in if you telephone them now.'

So Cheryl had done just that and so had missed
Rex calling. Davina had no idea how the situation
was between them so she decided to be diplomatic.

'Nice to see you,' she said with a smile. 'I'm afraid
Cheryl is out at the moment.'

Rex looked his usual expensive self, expensive
jeans, shirt and haircut. However, his usual jaunty
air was dimmed. He almost seemed relieved to
discover Cheryl was not there.

He said wryly, 'Not exactly a success, our visit to
Aunt Lila?'

'I wouldn't say that exactly. It was a change, and
we did eat.'

They both laughed and Davina twinkled, 'I was
just about to make coffee—will you have a cup?'

'About Cheryl,' said Rex as she refilled his cup.
'How does she feel about me?'

Davina handed him the plate of biscuits again and he helped himself.

'I haven't a clue. Why not ask her yourself? She'll be in soon,' she suggested.

He said ruminatively, 'You know, you're being awfully sweet to me. Why? I know you haven't much time for me.'

Davina shrugged. 'I've no right to be anything else, have I? You're Cheryl's boy-friend, not mine. Everyone has a right to live their life as they choose, but I must confess that I would interfere a little with Cheryl's or Darren's if I thought they were heading for disaster.'

Rex munched this with his biscuit. 'You think Cheryl is heading for disaster with me?'

'No one bettering themselves is exactly heading for disaster, although they might not, at the same time, be heading for happiness. I think happiness is the essential quality in life whether you're rich or poor.'

'What do you suggest?' he put in dryly. 'That I should give away my money, and live a hand-to-mouth existence?'

Davina laughed. 'Good heavens, no! Mind you, the experience might help you to mature, a quality that's essential in a married man.'

'Who said anything about marriage?'

Davina's eyes widened innocently. 'I hope that some day you intend to marry, but don't fool yourself that Cheryl is eager to marry you. I've no idea how she feels towards you. In any case, she can almost pick and choose in the matrimonial stakes. She's pretty enough and intelligent too.' She lifted her head as the door bell tinkled, and thrust her head between the beaded curtains separating the back room from the shop. 'Here she is now followed by a customer, so I'll leave you to it.'

Davina served several customers, and after looking at her watch realised that it was lunch time. Cheryl and Rex were still conversing earnestly in the back room and she made a sudden decision to eat out.

She stayed long enough to praise Cheryl's new hair-style and did not blame Rex for not being able to tear his eyes away from the sparkling blonde. Then she shed her overall, put on a short black velvet jacket and paused to alter the sign on the shop door from Open to Closed.

'Sorry, closed for lunch,' she informed the customer who bumped into her on her way out.

She smiled up past expensive soft leather shoes, long legs in immaculate trousers to wide shoulders and ... Nick.

'Good. You can have lunch with me. Come on.'

Taking her arm possessively between determinedly strong fingers, he marched her off to his parked car.

On breath regained, pulses hammering, Davina decided to play it cool.

'If you care to leave an order, sir, I'll make a note of it and attend to it later,' she gasped.

Darkly he said, 'Into the car before I beat you.'

He pushed her almost roughly into the yielding, well-sprung leather seat, and lost no time slipping in beside her behind the wheel.

He said equally roughly, 'You shouldn't have had that new hairstyle. You're taking an unfair advantage of me.'

Davina flashed him a startled look and said nothing.

'Here I am trying to forget you and you come right into my arms with a new look which absolutely floors me,' he went on harshly.

Her eyes flashed. 'Pot calling kettle black!' she cried. 'Here you are flaunting a handsome head of tight golden curls that any woman would give her ears for and you censure me for changing my hair-style. Of all the nerve!'

'That's nothing to do with it.' He took in the delicate curve of her cheek, the thick curling eye-lashes and the abundant shiny hair falling into natural waves. Then he looked down at the small-boned delicate wrists and ankles.

Davina did not speak nor look at him. While it was very flattering to know that she could attract him, she was afraid ... of him, of her own emotions. It was becoming extremely difficult to keep herself inviolate from his attacks on her armour.

To her frightened heart the air with him around was filled with gunpowder that was likely to explode at her first sign of weakness.

Wearily she said, 'You remind me of Rex. You have the same idea that anything you want you must have.'

Nick paused in the act of starting the car. 'And what's wrong with that providing you work to that end? It puts zip into life to set your sights on something and strive to that end.'

'A little unfair, though, when the dice are loaded in your favour with charm and good looks,' she protested.

'Most people can have charm and good looks if

they take the trouble to cultivate them. As for what you wear, while it helps, it is, after all, the expression you wear on your face, not the clothes you put on that counts,' he said sardonically.

'Do you know, I agree with you entirely.'

'Nice to know that we agree on something. Where would you like to eat?'

'I wasn't aware that I'd agreed to eat with you.'

He laughed. 'You have no other option—I'm much bigger than you are! I'll take you to my club. They've only recently begun to admit ladies —providing they're escorted by a member, of course.'

'Of course,' she echoed, and laughed.

It was nice to have V.I.P. treatment in a sanctum the very air of which bristled with males. The food was excellent, the wine of the very best and the service impeccable.

'You're very quiet,' Nick said over the coffee.

'I'm too replete with food. I've eaten too much,' she confessed.

'Nonsense, puff of wind would blow you away. Cigarette?'

He offered her his cigarette case and she refused. He lit a cigar for himself.

'I'd like to tell you a bit about myself,' he said carefully. 'My parents are away spending the winter in Florida. Mother had a bad bout of 'flu last year and Dad decided to take her away for the winter. They're missing the spring and aren't coming until summer is on the way.'

Davina smiled. 'I can't imagine you with parents. You're so self-contained. You don't seem to need anyone.'

'Well, I do, and I miss my parents like hell.' He leaned forward to tap ash from his cigar into an ashtray on the table. As he did so the rays of the sun slanting through the windows turned his hair to gold and Davina longed idiotically to run her fingers through the tight curls.

She said wistfully, 'Are your parents fair or dark?'

He grinned. 'Fair, both of them. I could say that Mother is the reason I've not married up to now. I've been looking for someone with her sentiments.'

Davina was aghast. 'But that isn't the way to marry and be happy. You have to fall in love first, and you certainly couldn't fall in love to order.'

He leaned across the table and looked audaciously into her eyes.

'Have you ever been in love?' he whispered.

The colour flooded to her face. She could have said that she was in love with him. Instead, she said flippantly,

'Unmarried girls are in love all the time with someone. I must disappoint you, though. I've had no affairs. For one thing I haven't had the time and for another I prefer to wait until the right man comes along.'

'But you've no time for him at the moment? You've found time to have a meal out today.'

She shrugged. 'I had a reason for eating out. Normally we have our lunch in the shop and cook a proper meal in the evening.'

'What happened, or shouldn't I ask?'

'I left Cheryl in the shop talking to Rex. They had a quarrel and I'm wondering now whether they're making it up again.'

'That was very generous of you. Tell me, don't you feel a little out of things when you see your younger sister enjoying the company of a boy-friend?'

'Sometimes. But I have dates, you know. My accountant takes me out sometimes. I'm also invited out for the evening by satisfied customers like your sister-in-law Juleen.'

'Ah yes, that reminds me. Her husband Jocelyn, a surgeon, who is also my brother, is coming home from a conference in the States soon. By then the parents will also be back, so we can have a get-together. I don't know if Juleen has told you, but they're living in Paris at the moment.'

'That will be nice for you.'

His look at her was guarded. 'I'm hoping that you and I will know each other better by then.'

Davina's heart gave a lurch. 'In what way?'

'We shall be going steady by then.'

She shook her head. 'I don't think so. I've far too much to do at the shop to form any permanent attachments.'

'You can dine with me occasionally, go to a show or for a run in the car. We might even get together at Juleen's place or Lila's. Rex's aunt and uncle are friends of mine.'

'I'm sorry.'

He jabbed out the cigar on the ash tray. 'Don't be such a little coward,' he said quietly. 'You're obviously frightened to death of me, aren't you?'

'No, I'm not. I'm not going to be pushed around, that's all, and I do have responsibilities.'

'Cheryl and Darren? What if Cheryl marries her Rex? Then you only have Darren. That's where I come in. He'll have a big elder brother who will listen to all his problems.'

'No, Nick, it wouldn't work. You and I are better parting here and now. I'm going to see this thing through if it kills me.'

He stared at her for several moments with narrowed eyes.

'If that's the way you want it, my sweet, then so be it.'

He had taken his dismissal so calmly that she felt piqued in spite of herself. It seemed at first from the expression in his grey eyes that he could not believe it. Probably no woman had ever refused his friendship before. It was certainly a blow to his ego, but Davina felt it was a hollow victory.

He drove her back to the shop and dropped her off without a word. Then with a lift of a hand he had gone.

Cheryl had not returned from lunch, which presumably she too had eaten out. With Rex? It was more than likely. Had she also given him the brush-off? If Cheryl had then she would not tell her sister about it—Davina was sure of that.

Something was eating Cheryl. If it wasn't Rex then who or what was it? Nick?

Cheryl came in around two-thirty. 'Hello there,' she said. 'Why did you go out for lunch on your own? You could have gone with Rex and me.'

Davina raised pretty arched brows. 'And played gooseberry?' she cried derisively. 'Why did you think I left you alone?'

Cheryl slipped out of her jacket and hung it on a coat hanger behind the beaded curtain.

'We've made up. Rex wants me to get engaged,' she said quietly.

Davina stared at the sober expression. 'Really, I can't see you dancing around the room in glee. Where's the ring?'

Cheryl shrugged. 'There isn't one yet. I told him I'd think about it. There's no hurry.'

'For someone who's been dreaming of marriage, I must say you're playing it cool. Aren't you sure of your feelings for him, or is there someone else?' Davina said dryly.

'There's no one else. I suppose I'll get round to being Rex's one and only love.'

Davina smiled fondly at her sister. 'I'm glad you're being sensible about it and making sure. The last thing I want you to do it to make a wrong decision where your future is concerned. Darren's too. I have nightmares about you both sometimes. I could never be happy myself if you two aren't happy as well. I'd feel that I'd failed the parents. They loved us all so much and Darren was Mother's special pet. So you have to be sure, Cheryl, in your choice of a partner.'

Davina put the used coffee cups left earlier in the tiny sink and washed her hands. Reaching for the hand towel, she was aware of her sister standing in front of the wall mirror patting her hair into place.

'Nothing on your mind, Cheryl, have you?' she queried.

The answer came far too quickly for it to be entirely truthful.

'Of course I haven't, and I wish you'd stop treating Darren and me like a couple of kids,' Cheryl snapped.

Davina winced inwardly at the sharpness of her tone. It was so unlike her sister to go off at the deep end at the slightest provocation.

'There is something wrong, isn't there?' she insisted. 'Is it Nick Tabor?'

Cheryl swung round on her with heightened colour.

'No, it isn't. You know very well it's you he's interested in.'

'Oh!' Davina recovered herself quickly. 'Well, even if he is you could still like him, couldn't you?'

'You're wrong.' Cheryl presented her back. 'I'm sorry to fly off like that. I didn't mean it,' she mumbled. 'You're so good to Darren and me, always putting us first. We do appreciate it.'

Davina went to place an arm around the slender shoulders.

'I'm sorry if at times I've been overbearing—it's just that I want the best out of life for all of us. I know it's a tall order, but I'm going to do my best, and you both have to help me,' Davina said gently. 'As the eldest it's my responsibility.'

Cheryl spoke so low that Davina had to listen carefully.

'There are times when I wish you hadn't bought the shop. We all ought to have taken our share of the money and gone our own ways.'

'But how could you? How could Darren? He wouldn't have bothered with an education and what would you have done?'

'I might have married Rex,' defiantly.

'What's stopping you from doing so now? For goodness' sake, Cheryl, what's got into you?'

'Forget it.'

At the sound of the shop door opening Cheryl went quickly into the shop.

Davina's spirit wilted. She had schooled herself to doing her best in the role of mother since her parents had gone. In a way she had known that it would be a thankless task. Not that either Cheryl or Darren were bad. Like all teenagers they were headstrong and impulsive.

It was true, as she had said, that they would have both gone through their money like water. But the knowledge that this was so did little to act as balm to her hurt. However, there was the shop and if it did well it would be the means of making their legacy from their parents more substantial.

As a medical student, Darren would need a small regular income on the side to augment his grant. As always Davina whipped her flagging spirit. One thing she was determined to do in the future was to go out more herself in order not to get into a rut.

A week or so went by with things going normally. Cheryl seemed to have recovered and was her own bright self. Davina put it down to them both being under par since their illness. Cheryl went out with Rex and Davina went out herself at least twice a week.

She was not short of dates, but she kept them casual. Nick crept into her thoughts constantly, but the passing days were an ever-increasing mist shutting him out.

Then one day he telephoned her. He was picking her up for lunch. Just like that, and there was nothing she could do about it since it was early closing day.

As it happened Cheryl was out for the day with Rex. They had gone to the races. Thursday morning was usually a slack period and it was a beautiful day.

After the telephone call Davina found herself continually consulting her watch and as the time drew near for lunch she got the jitters. Wildly she thought of going out the back way in order to avoid Nick. No customers came after twelve-thirty and she was ready well before one o'clock. Even so she hung about.

The blare of his horn sounding like a command roused her. He had climbed out of the car, unfolding his long legs and raising a hand in greeting as she left the shop. He opened the car door for her and she smiled at his provocative grin.

Her spirits lifted as he slid in beside her behind the wheel. His grey eyes were twinkling. The quirk of his well cut mouth made her stomach turn upside down as he leaned towards her.

'Miss me?'

So much, because I loved you beyond all thinking or logic. However, none of the words were spoken aloud, and he did not wait for an answer.

'Are you free?' he asked politely.

'I'm free,' she answered, and gave a sweet twinkling laugh.

He started the car and nosed through the traffic. 'I have a little pub in mind where they do special roast beef sandwiches to have with a good glass of beer. Or would you prefer a restaurant with waiters hovering?'

'The pub, please. It sounds delicious.'

As he drove she glanced at the clear-cut profile and the cap of tightly curled hair trimmed into neat wisps at his neck. The hands on the wheel, well tended, looked strong and firm. Idiotically, she looked for some change in him since they had last met and found none.

The magic of his presence was as strong as ever, so was the usual need for few words between them. All too soon Nick was slowing down into a car park and ushering her into an oak-beamed jewel of a pub impregnated with the smell of well polished wood and beer barrels.

They went to a well polished table in a corner by a window and the waiter brought their order.

Nick lifted his glass to hers. 'Cheers,' he said. 'You're looking great. There isn't a discordant note about you.'

'I could say the same for you,' she said. 'Why this interest in me all of a sudden?'

He made a pretence of being hurt. 'Don't you think I've been very kind in leaving you alone?'

Davina listened to the beating of her own treacherous heart. She ached with loving him so much. Her love had been like a nocturnal animal quietly sleeping until he had jogged it back into life.

Her small white teeth sank into the delicious sandwich. What utter bliss it was to sit leisurely for once in no hurry to go anywhere. The daffodils in the centre of the table were caught in the same beam of sunlight slanting on Nick's well-shaped head from the window. His eyelashes were thick and golden as were the fine hairs on the backs of his hands.

She giggled suddenly and he looked at her narrow-eyed.

'Sorry,' she said. 'I couldn't possibly tell you why I laughed.'

He had demolished his sandwich and reached for another.

'You're laughing because you're happy to be here with me? Right?'

She shook her head. 'No. Wrong.'

'Then I insist upon knowing why you were laughing,' he warned her darkly. 'You're living dangerously, my girl.'

'You asked for it, and it's your fault if I embarrass you. I was thinking what a good thing it is that you aren't dark. You'd look terribly hairy.'

'Ah yes, you prefer dark men.'

Davina sighed. 'I'm afraid it's something I grew up with. Someone dark, dashing and daring.'

'Hypocrite,' he teased. 'You'd run a mile from anyone who was dashing and daring.'

'I would not!'

Davina had cider with her lunch. It was the most enjoyable day she had ever spent. Nick took her for a run in the country after lunch, and a good hour's driving brought them to tree-lined country roads and the sweet smell of summer.

Parking the car in a layby, he took her hand and walked with her to a grassy knoll surrounded by trees where he spread his jacket on the ground for her to sit down.

With the birds singing in the trees above them and the muted sound of traffic on a motorway in the distance, Davina lay on her back to squint up at the blue sky.

'Heavenly, isn't it, to take a break and return to sanity away from the jungle of concrete?' she murmured.

Using her folded arms to cast a shade on her face from the eye-watering sky, she laughed up at him. Too late she saw her mistake.

Catching hold of her wrists and drawing her arms down on either side of her, he bent over her lips.

'No, Nick. Behave yourself!' She struggled.

'I am behaving myself very nicely, and keep still.'

She turned her head away quickly and his kiss landed on the side of her neck. Then his lips sought the hollow between her breast and she turned her head back in sudden revolt.

Her second mistake. He took her lips gently at first. Her brain reeled as he drew her tight against him, and her lips responded to the deepening pressure of his. She was fast losing her resistance as her body grew limp against his harder one.

Then the peal of girlish laughter came from a long distance away sounding just like Cheryl, and she struggled to free herself. She grew rigid and, gradually, Nick let her go.

'It's ... no use ... Nick,' she gasped. 'Let's go.'

He stared down at her as though she was some mathematical problem that he had a difficulty in solving.

Harshly he said, 'I told you you were a hypocrite. All this talk about a dashing and daring hero. What are you made of anyway?'

He sprang to his feet and walked away a short distance to stare over the rural landscape, presenting his wide shoulders to her anguished gaze.

She sat up and cried helplessly, 'I'm sorry, Nick. You ... you wouldn't understand. Cheryl doesn't either.'

Her voice grew more and more wobbly as she struggled on to talk to his unyielding back. Then, to her own dismay, she began to weep silently into her hands.

Instantly Nick was kneeling beside her, taking hold of her slender wrists to draw her hands down from her face.

'There's nothing to cry about,' he said gruffly. 'Here, take my handkerchief and dry your tears. Here—blow. Then we can talk in the car.'

Davina blew her nose and with his arm around her walked with him to the car. He had thrown his jacket over one shoulder to leave the other arm free to place around her.

At the car he helped her in, slipped on his jacket and sat beside her.

'Have you fallen out with Cheryl?' he asked.

She shook her head. 'Not really.'

'By the way, has she made it up with Rex?'

'Yes. He wants her to get engaged. She's thinking about it.'

He shook his head. 'Dear, dear, these Mawne sisters are sure hard to drag to the altar!'

Indignantly, Davina said, 'Cheryl isn't yet seventeen.'

'She needs someone to look after her. Hasn't that occurred to you?'

'It occurs to me all the time.'

He said wryly, 'You need someone to look after you too.'

'I'm doing very well as I am. I do my best.'

'Of course you do.' He shifted in his seat to turn and face her. 'But you're only a couple of babes.'

'We'll grow up, and now will you take me home?'

Nick made no move. His tones were ragged. 'You'll burn yourself out in the process. What's wrong in having a husband's broad shoulders to cry on? Women alone are always at a disadvantage —I'm sure you don't need me to tell you that.'

Davina looked up at him frankly. He was much too near and it was so easy to weaken. She loved him, there was no doubt about that, but there was Cheryl. If her sister was in love with him as she suspected then how would she react to a friendship that would only result in marriage breaking up the family?

Cheryl might easily marry Rex on the rebound, and what kind of a marriage would that be? Her hands were clasped tightly in her lap and she gazed down on them helplessly. They would be tied if she married. Right now they were free.

'I don't want you to tell me anything. I want to go on as I've been doing until I see this thing through,' she murmured stonily.

'But it might take years—years that you could never recall to enrich your own life. You need a husband and children. Are you going to deny yourself the things that matter to a woman? Are you always going to be on the outside looking in on other people's happiness?'

The eyes she lifted to his were clear and resigned.

'If that's how it has to be, yes. I don't think it will, though. I think if you do what you think to be the right thing something comes for you.'

He laughed then groaned. 'My sweet, what am I to do with you? I could be that certain something that has come to you. I'm going to see you whether you want it or not. You're going to have me around for a very long time, but I might as well tell you that I'm not a very patient man when I want something very much.'

He bent to kiss the tip of her nose. 'I asked you to a sandwich lunch because this evening you're going out with me to a party.' His eyes had steely glints in them at the shake of her head, and he went on, 'I shall call for you at seven o'clock—and you'd better be ready.'

He started the car, muttered something unprintable under his breath as a motorist travelling at an excessive speed came too far over the layby to miss them by inches, and drove on.

One thing that Davina had discovered about Nick was the fact that he never sulked. Soon he was talking about things he knew would interest her, funny incidents on his travels abroad, of which there were many.

Soon he had her laughing helplessly, unaware of him getting under her guard. Wiping tears of mirth from her eyes, it had almost been her undoing as she cried weakly, 'Oh, Nick, I . . .'

She had been on the verge of saying, I love you, and stopped in time.

'Yes?' he prompted. 'Finish what you were going to say.'

'It . . . er . . . it was nothing important,' she stam-

mered, thankful that he did not take his eyes from
the road to see her telltale blush.

'Don't forget. Seven this evening.'

Those were his last words when he dropped her
off at the flat over the shop. Cheryl had not come
back when Davina washed and dressed to go out
with Nick that evening. Being on her own had
given her time to look at things in their true per-
spective.

She could manage without Nick, but if she did
then she had to come to terms with this terrible feeling of being isolated not only from her small family
but from everything else. Like Nick had said, being
an onlooker while other people lived.

Dear Nick! He was everything she wanted in a
man—exciting, witty, dashing, daring with a won-
derfully built body which made her feel weak with
primitive needs which frightened her.

Her decision to go out with him again brought its
own difficulties of how she was going to keep him in
check. He was a virile and full-blooded man who
could, no doubt, discipline his own desires up to a
certain point.

Davina had a bath, slipped on fine underwear and
a dress utterly feminine in its swirl of frothy ele-
gance. Her newly washed hair was fragrant and soft
as silk. The glow on the creamy delicate skin of her
face had a radiance inspired by thoughts of seeing
Nick.

She was ready when he called, tripping out to him
with a wrap around her slenderness that gave her an
ethereal look.

Tall, rangy with an impression of curly fair hair,
and grey eyes that stared right through her, Nick,

heartbreakingly handsome in evening dress, helped her into the car.

It took her an age to collect herself, to put up her armour against that handsome arrogance that was so mind-shrivelling and dangerous to her.

At last she said lightly, 'You haven't told me where we're going.'

'Juleen's place,' he replied laconically.

'Does she know you're bringing me?'

He raised a brow. 'I don't, as a rule, describe the girl I take to her parties.'

'That isn't what I mean and you know it!'

'I haven't the least idea what you're talking about,' he replied with maddening calmness. 'You like Juleen, don't you?'

'Of course I do, but she's far better off than I am and we don't move in the same circle of friends.'

'Nonsense! You're going as my guest.'

The party was in full swing when they arrived. The room was jam-packed with people swaying together to the music from a record player.

Nick met her gaze with a grimace. 'Want to go?' he asked, extricating her from between two groups of people who stood chatting over drinks.

Quivering at the thought of being in some dim intimate place with him, Davina shook her head emphatically. It was then that Juleen bore down upon them.

Agitatedly, she caught Nick by the arm. 'Glad you've come,' she told him with heightened colour. 'We have gatecrashers—about two dozen of them over there by the door.'

A scruffy gang of youngsters were tipping back drinks and dancing in one corner of the room. They were making a terrific noise and Nick's face set.

'I'll soon get rid of them,' he said grimly.

'Do be careful!' Juleen wrung her hands nervously as she spoke, but Nick was already shouldering his way through the guests.

Davina turned her back and refused to look as Juleen appeared to notice her for the first time.

'Hello, Davina,' she said. 'Did you come with Nick?'

'Yes.'

Juleen looked at her thoughtfully. 'Is Nick dating you?' she asked abruptly.

'He's trying to,' she admitted.

'Trying to?' Juleen echoed. 'That's unusual for Nick. He normally has no trouble in persuading girls to go out with him.'

'I can quite believe it,' Davina said wryly.

Juleen smiled. 'Are you playing hard to get?' she queried sweetly.

'No.'

'Just cautious? I don't blame you.'

Davina sensed an atmosphere. 'I have a feeling that you don't approve of me going with Nick.'

Juleen's smile was enigmatic. 'Let's say you're a nice girl who expects marriage, and Nick ... he just isn't the marrying kind.' She shrugged bare shoulders. 'I've introduced him to the most beautiful girls and he's never taken any of them seriously.'

'Perhaps he hasn't met the right one yet. In any case I haven't anything as tying as marriage in mind at the moment. I've too many commitments at home,' Davina assured her.

To her relief Nick came back in that moment, having got rid of the gatecrashers. Both women looked at him anxiously as he grinned.

Davina said, 'No black eyes?'

'Disappointed?' he drawled.

Juleen said playfully, 'That was very clever of you. Where are they, and how did you manage it so quickly?'

His grey eyes held a wicked twinkle. 'I told them there was a much better party next door.'

Juleen was suddenly convulsed with laughing. 'The two Daker brothers?' she croaked in glee.

'Who are they?' Davina asked.

Nick's mouth tilted humorously. 'Two outsize wrestlers.'

That night was the beginning of their friendship. She agreed to meet with him once a week, at lunch time, when he was in town.

CHAPTER FIVE

NICK had been away on business for three weeks. Davina knew that she would miss him, but had never guessed just how much. Work at the shop became a daily routine. Cheryl was going out with Rex still minus a ring and Davina pored over the accounts.

Everyone except herself was involved in some highly personal activity. She ached to see Nick again, longed for his touch.

Weekend came and after lunch on Sunday she went up to sunbathe on the roof of the flat. She had spread the towel out under her and had closed her eyes.

Someone coming on to the roof awakened her. Cheryl had gone out for the day with Rex. Davina sat up half asleep as someone sat down beside her.

'Nick!' she cried in delighted surprise, then lowered her eyelids in case her eyes gave her away.

'Please to see me?' he asked. 'I've missed you like hell.'

Putting his arms around her, he set his mouth to hers in no uncertain manner, kissing her so thoroughly that they both fell flat on the towel.

Davina was suddenly alive from top to toe as she clung, unable to let go. She thrust her fingers through the tight curls clustering around his well shaped head as he drew her fiercely against him. Her love for him, battened down for so long, rose into a flaring need.

'You've got to marry me, Davina, or I can't answer for the consequences,' he muttered against her lips.

She closed her eyes. The world was receding. There was no further resistance in her as she succumbed to the wild beating of her heart. His lips moved down to the low neck of her swimsuit. Her swimsuit! Her receding senses were abruptly reminded of her state of undress, and they brought her back to reality like the shock of cold water.

She began to struggle wildly, wrenching herself free. She must have been mad! It was a madness that would return as soon as his arms were around her again. She knew that.

Her only instinct was to escape from what was an impossible situation. She loved him and knew that he loved her. They had proved to be two passionate people whose love would, if encouraged, defy all the conventions. A platonic friendship was impossible between them, and marriage was out.

'Davina.'

He made to take her again in his arms, but the next instant she had rolled away from him and was on her feet. Nick rose as quickly and was gripping her shoulders.

'For heaven's sake, what's the matter?' he demanded.

She saw his face through a blur of tears and blinked them away hastily.

'Please let me go, Nick,' she pleaded huskily.

Already the touch of his hands on her bare shoulders was undermining her defences, and she shivered as he obeyed.

Bending to pick up the towel, she placed it

around her swim suit. Raising her eyes no higher than his firm jaw, she said, 'It's no use. I told you I'm not free.'

He placed a firm finger beneath her chin and raised her face.

'Don't you love me?' he demanded.

'That's nothing to do with it. I know what I have to do and marriage is out, so is any demanding friendship, and I know the latter is impossible between you and me.'

'You're darned right it is. I'm mad about you. Do you know that? Every mannerism, the way you turn your head, the graceful way you walk, the expressive movements of your lovely hands closing around my heart drive me mad with longing for you.' His eyes burned down at her. 'I waken in the night wishing like hell that you're there beside me. Doesn't that mean anything to you?'

Her green eyes were blank with despair and she looked at him wordlessly. He was gripping her shoulders again and for a moment she was sure that he was going to shake her. His teeth were clamped together, and his breathing was deep, and dangerous.

She swallowed on an obstruction in her throat. She loved him so much. It would have been heaven to hand over the reins to him, to let him take her worries on his broad shoulders. But there was her family.

'Please don't let's talk about it,' she begged, then frowned as something occurred to her. 'How did you get into the flat?' she asked.

'I met Cheryl and Rex,' laconically.

She focussed wide green eyes on his set dark face.

'And Cheryl gave you her key just like that?' she gasped.

He smiled grimly. 'I asked her for it because she told me you were spending the weekend at home.'

Davina swung herself out of his grasp and made for the exit to the flat below.

Nick followed hot on her heels and confronted her in the pleasant lounge.

'What do you intend to do about us?' he demanded grimly.

'Please, Nick, don't touch me. I can't think clearly when you do.'

Davina stepped back as he would have taken her into his arms. Her brain was reeling as Cheryl's words came back to her in full force. What she had said about the right man coming along had been true, and that she could so easily miss out on him.

Nick smiled, a smile that did not reach his eyes. 'That's something. It means you care for me as I care for you. Oh, my darling, stop dithering and leave everything to me.'

He took her into his arms and claimed her quivering lips. Poor Davina needed all her strength to resist him.

'Nick, let me go!' she cried as he pulled the towel from her shoulders. 'And stop playing games.'

The next moment they were both staring towards the lounge door as someone entered.

'Darren!' Davina gasped. 'What are you doing here? Have you come for the day?'

He came in looking slightly dishevelled, flinging an antagonistic glance at Nick.

'I expected you and Cheryl to be out,' he said

ungraciously. 'I didn't expect to find you with a visitor.'

Davina smiled warmly. 'Why not, it's the weekend. Go and clean up I'll get you something to eat when I've changed. I know you're always hungry after a journey.'

He slouched away to his room and she looked helplessly at Nick.

'I must go and change and get a meal for Darren.'

'In other words, would I mind leaving? I'll go, but only on condition that you have lunch with me at least once a week. That isn't asking too much, is it?'

She nodded. 'Wednesday.'

'Thursday, your half day,' he told her inexorably. 'I'll pick you up.'

He had gone before she could make a protest. She stood there for some seconds staring into space, then with a deep sigh she made her way sadly to her room.

Darren had eaten up everything Davina had prepared for him and was now stretching his long legs out contentedly before him as he lighted a cigarette.

'How long have you been smoking?' she asked, gathering up the used dishes and taking them to the sink to be washed later.

He sent out a line of smoke to the kitchen ceiling and his very youth made her feel a hundred years old. He was in the stages of growing up and she had to let him do some things his own way. Smoking was one of them.

'Not long. I don't smoke a lot—can't afford to. Are you going to marry him?'

Davina put the last of the dishes in the sink and swung round.

'Marry who? You mean Nick?'

He shrugged. 'Who else? Cheryl told me that he's nuts about you.'

'Cheryl is too romantic for words. Come on into the lounge where you can be more comfortable.'

She led the way out of the kitchen and Darren threw himself into a comfortable chair, tossing one long leg over the arm.

'Well, are you going to marry him?' he insisted.

Davina ruffled his dark hair and went to sit facing him on the settee.

'Would it matter very much to you if I did?' she queried.

He frowned. 'Of course it would. It wouldn't be home any more, would it, with a stranger in it?'

She said gently, 'Nick wouldn't be a stranger. He'd be my husband and your brother-in-law.'

Obstinately, he insisted, 'He would still be de trop. Don't get me wrong—I'm not against you having boy-friends. In fact I'm surprised you haven't had more than you have. A girl as pretty as you must have some wolves prowling around.'

'Nick isn't a wolf. He's very nice when you know him. I'm not going to marry him, if that's what's worrying you. But it isn't, is it? Why exactly did you come today, Darren? If you'd been coming for the weekend you would have been here yesterday. Have you been roughing it?'

He studied the glowing end of the cigarette he was smoking.

'I've been wondering whether it's worth while going on with medicine. I'm going to be studying for years. I just had to get away for a while.' He laughed. 'I slept under the stars last night.'

Davina looked at him in horror. 'But why? Don't tell me you're going to be another of those idiot students who end up bashing the world about and find that the only thing they've been bashing is themselves.'

'No. I'm just undecided, that's all.'

She smiled in relief. 'Then you're not a mixed-up kid, thank goodness?'

'No, definitely not.'

'Then if you want my advice you'll continue with your studies until you've made up your mind what you want to do. I'll be willing to help you whatever it is you decide.'

'That's fine.' The worried look vanished from his face. 'You know, it's great having a home to come to and someone who cares. I'm glad you're not going to marry yet. Want a hand with the dishes?'

Weeks passed, with Davina lunching with Nick often when he was in town. Then came a period of time when he was away; long unsettling weeks when the flower shop lost its appeal and became an all-absorbing trap imprisoning her.

Each day stretched endlessly ahead bringing with it the usual routine jobs, the errands, and problems. One day was more or less like another with twelve or fourteen hours to fill before the day was partly through. Afterwards, the flat was as good as any place to be.

Then one evening he telephoned her from the airport. He was driving from there to the flat to take her out to dinner. Davina was tense. She had longed for this moment, but now it was here it was too immediate, too overwhelming.

Idiot, she called herself in disgust. Do I want to see him or don't I? She was waiting when he arrived, dressed and ready.

With a look which made her heart turn over, he said,

'We've a lot of time to make up for, my sweet.'

He took her out to dinner to gaze at her across the table with a look in his eyes which made her tremble, and they stayed for the cabaret despite her protests that he must be very tired after his journey from abroad.

He had kissed her fingers across the dining table and his lips had brushed her hair when he had helped her on with her wrap. But later when driving home he made for the open country and stopped in a quiet spot as she had known he would in order to have his own way.

When he released her she was battling for breath. The shocked fear registering on her hot face was on account of the knowledge of her own weakness in her love for him. She had no armour against him. His nearness, his kisses reduced her to a puppet who danced at his will.

His grey eyes were hard as granite. 'If you feared my kisses so much why did you come out with me?' he demanded savagely. 'What did you expect after being away from you for so long? I think this has gone on long enough, don't you?'

Davina turned her head away from his piercing eyes. A hand half wandered upwards to touch her bruised lips, then landed half way, against his chest.

'You needn't hold me off,' he went on, his voice

still on ice. 'I shan't be kissing you again. I'd better take you home.'

Outside the flat he prevented her from leaving the car by leaning over her and holding the door catch.

'When is it going to be, Davina? I know you love me. You wouldn't pretend about that. We have to marry.'

His face was very near to her own. Davina felt the need in him reaching out to the same need in her.

'Oh, Nick!' she breathed, framing his face in her hands. Then her hands were no longer around his face but curling around his neck with all her slender suppleness pressed against him. He was kissing her gently; tasting the salt of her tears and all her sweetness; feeling her tight against his leaping heart as his lips found hers in a long moment of ecstasy.

'You are going to marry me, aren't you, my sweet?' he whispered after long ardent moments had passed. 'How soon?'

'Please can we be engaged for a while first? I have a reason for asking. And ... and can we keep it a secret from Darren? For a while, until I can explain to him?'

He frowned down at her pleading eyes. 'Anything you say as long as you marry me. But why this secrecy from Darren? He doesn't bully you, does he, my darling?'

'No. Oh no! But it isn't long since we lost our parents and Darren feels that little bit unsure. He needs an anchor. He needs to feel wanted. I ... I can't explain really. Please don't rush me, Nick.'

His arms slackened enough for him to look down

into her face. As though being tolerant against his will, he said,

'I'm not waiting long after the engagement party.'

'Must we have an engagement party?'

'We could get married right away, if that's what you want.'

'You know that isn't what I want.' She strained back a little in his hold. 'I think we ought to know each other a little more before we decide anything as serious as marriage, don't you?'

He said impatiently, 'And how much better will we know each other meeting as we do? I know what I want—you. I'm sure you feel the same about me.'

'Yes, I do. I love you very much.'

'I still don't understand why you can't let Darren know you're getting engaged, Davina,' Cheryl said as they dressed for the engagement party. 'He wouldn't be able to come in any case because of his studies.'

'That's the trouble. I want to see him and talk to him about it before he knows. That's also why I'm keeping on the shop after I'm married. Darren wouldn't take kindly to being assisted in his studies by my husband. It wouldn't be the same. There is such a thing as pride.'

'I still think you're wrong in not letting him know. Nick is sure to send the announcement of your engagement to the newspapers, and it's bound to be an important affair.'

'Not all that important. We're having the party at Juleen Tabor's flat. Her husband will be there to make it more of a family affair.'

Davina stepped into a delicious pure silk dress in creamy white, flower-patterned, with shoulder straps and a full skirt billowing out from her tiny waist. An excellent affair which seemed exclusively designed for the deep-fringed hand-embroidered silk shawl she was to wear with it.

Cheryl's dress in midnight blue was equally enchanting. Rex was collecting her in his car and Nick was picking Davina up in his. Cheryl had already gone when Nick arrived, ringing the door bell with all the persistence of an impatient lover.

The evening dress set off his mocking dark face, his wide shoulders and the lean-loined vigour of his movements as he strode in to gaze at her appraisingly.

Davina backed at the hungry look in his eyes as he openly adored her.

'Now, now,' she cried. 'No upsetting my hair. I'm all ready.'

But he only laughed and hauled her into his arms to kiss her until she had to push him away. He took it all in good part.

'Just wait until we're married, that's all,' he threatened darkly.

'It won't be a big affair, will it, Nick?' she asked apprehensively.

'Stop worrying,' he replied. 'I'm the one who should be worrying, about how to keep you at bay from the wolves. You'll be the belle of the ball. I can't stop looking at you. I can't believe my luck. You're so sweet and feminine, I just want to eat you up.'

Davina did not know what she expected in the way of guests, but the elegant gathering brought home to her the circle that Nick moved in through his position as an international banker.

Immediately she began to have qualms that were dispelled a little upon meeting Nick's brother Jocelyn. Not as tall as Nick, with brown hair and eyes, he had an air of calm about him that radiated warmth and confidence.

'I've been looking forward to meeting you, Davina,' he said cordially, taking her hand. 'I couldn't wait to see the girl who had really managed to pierce the cynical armour of brother Nick. He isn't the kind to go overboard for any woman—he's much too disciplined. Anyway, you have yourself a fine man, one of the best.'

Nick was chatting with Juleen, who seemed to be over the moon to have her husband home. She was wearing a figure-hugging dress in smoke grey velvet. Davina watched as Nick flicked a lighter to the inevitable cigarette Juleen had made part of her.

'My wife smokes far too much,' Jocelyn said close to her ear. 'I've left her to her own devices far too long. By the way, who is that young man just come in? Do you know him?'

The colour left Davina's face leaving her pale and agitated.

'My brother Darren,' she said in a voice strangely unlike her own. 'Excuse me.

'Hello, Darren. I . . . I didn't think you'd be able to take time off,' she stammered. 'Who told you?'

His look was distinctly hostile. 'Is there somewhere where we can talk?' he asked tight-lipped.

Davina looked around the gathering of well-dressed men and women, meeting Cheryl's eyes across the room as she did so. Cheryl's shake of the head clearly indicated that she was not the one who had told Darren of the engagement.

But the knowledge that her sister had not let her down did nothing to calm Davina, who caught her brother's arm and guided him through the guests to Juleen's study.

The party had not yet got underway as they passed through a room converted into a bar and on to the place Davina had in mind. To her relief it was empty of people as she closed the door behind Darren's stiffly erect figure.

'Well,' he challenged, shoving his hands into his pockets and glaring at her. 'So you aren't going to marry. Full stop!'

'Don't stand glaring at me like an avenging angel, Darren! Sit down. I was going to tell you eventually. I didn't ask you to the engagement party because I wanted to explain first.'

'Explain what? That we're going to have a new boss in the family? Well, you can count me out!'

Davina quivered. 'What do you mean?'

He strolled to lean back against the heavy desk and Davina grasped the back of a chair to face him.

'I mean you can give me my share of the parents' legacy and I'll clear out.'

Davina's knuckles as she grasped the chair back were as white as her face.

He went on, 'I counted on you, but you let me down just like the parents did. I might be younger than you, but I am the man of the house.'

'That's true,' Davina conceded. 'But the parents didn't leave enough to see you through medical school. So I invested the money wisely and in time it will bring in good returns along with the proceeds from the flower shop. As the investment is long-term it will be very difficult to give you your share right away. Besides, I don't intend to. In your present mood you're liable to blow the lot.'

Darren went red, then white. 'You can borrow the money from your rich boy-friend. It seems that from now on he's going to be the piper who calls the tune,' he sneered.

'What we have has nothing to do with Nick. I shall keep the shop on after I'm married and things will be as they were before.'

'How can they be?' he scoffed. 'Next thing will be Cheryl getting married. What about the happy home then? What do I do, take over the vacant flat or move in with some friend?'

'I'm not married yet, neither is Cheryl. You're jumping fences that simply aren't there. Look, Darren, I love you too much to see you unhappy. I'll ... call the whole thing off if it distresses you.'

'And where would that put me?' he demanded angrily. 'I'd be referred to as the monster who'd wrecked your life. No, thanks. I'll take what money I can get and hop it, seeing how I'm cluttering up your life.'

'Now you're being as young as you are,' retorted Davina. 'You're behaving like the spoilt brat you've always been. Mother made a young god of you, but now you have to work for what you have like I have to do. I worked twelve hours a day on that small-holding in order to give us all a good start in life. That's what our parents wanted for us, and that's what you're going to have!'

They glared at each other like opponents fighting to the death, but with Davina anger could never last for long, especially against those she loved.

'Please, Darren, give yourself a chance. I won't close the shop, neither shall I allow Nick to have any say in our affairs. All the help you need in your education and after will be money from the estate. That way you'll never owe any part of your career to anyone but your own parents.'

Her voice had been gently pleading and the tears in her eyes begged him to listen to reason. But before he could answer Nick strode into the room followed by his brother Jocelyn.

'There you are,' cried Nick with a grin. 'I wondered where you'd got to. Darren, I want you to meet my brother Jocelyn. He's a brain surgeon, so you should have a lot in common. Jocelyn, Davina's younger brother now at medical school, Darren Mawne.'

Davina stood dumbfounded. It was all too clear now to her that Nick had sent for Darren. How dared he without telling her? It was just the kind of high-handed thing he would do! Giving him a look which spoke volumes, she swept from the room, to bump into Juleen.

'Can you tell me where Jocelyn and Nick have got to?' Juleen asked anxiously. 'Everyone is about to go into the buffet room.' She glanced at Davina's ashen expression. 'Is anything wrong? You look quite pale, Davina, otherwise you're a vision of loveliness—beautiful dress, my dear.'

Davina managed a smile. 'All the excitement,' she explained.

Juleen patted her shoulder. 'Nick is a darling, isn't he? I should imagine it is more than exciting being engaged to him. There'll be more than a few envious looks in your direction tonight and in Nick's as well.'

'Thanks.' Davina went in search of Cheryl, whom she found in a small crowd of young people.

'Rex has gone to look for you,' Cheryl whispered, pulling Davina to one side. 'We're about to go into the buffet. I didn't send for Darren. Where is he, by the way?'

'With Nick and his brother Jocelyn,' Davina told her grimly. 'Just wait until I get my hands on Nick!'

'You mean Nick fetched Darren here? I can't believe it!' Cheryl cried in surprise. 'What would he want to do a thing like that for? Darren is no fan of Nick's.'

'That's what I intend to find out,' Davina told her darkly. 'Here he is now.'

Cheryl followed her gaze to where Nick was striding towards them across the room.

As she watched his loose-limbed grace as he crossed the room Davina's treacherous heart leapt out to meet him. This is no time to dwell upon his undoubted charms, she admonished herself sternly, and hardened her heart.

'Nick——' she began.

He stopped her with a quick gesture. 'We have very little time, so come with me,' he commanded, taking her hand.

Davina tried to draw her hand from his grasp, only to discover how deceptive the lightness of his grip was. Part of her was ready to say bitter cutting things about his high-handedness while the other part told her that it would only take one step into his arms.

She found herself being borne along swiftly to a guest bedroom and prepared for some plain speaking.

'What do you mean?' she began immediately the door was closed on their privacy. 'How dare you send for Darren! You've spoiled everything!'

Tears brightened the green of her eyes and she brushed them away angrily.

'Hey now!' he exclaimed in dismay. 'Not tears? I did it for you.'

'For me? You must be joking!'

He took her arm and led her to a roomy, comfortable chair into which he sank down to pull her on to his knees.

'Now tell me what's on your mind,' he said gently, holding her against him.

Her voice was muffled against his chest. 'I was going to explain to Darren in a way he could understand, and ... and now you've spoiled it all. He's angry, and it's through you!'

He kissed her hair. 'My dear girl, you've got it all wrong. I'm no fool and I knew something like this would happen, so I decided to protect you as far as I could.'

She lifted her head to glare at him indignantly. 'Protect me? In what way?' she cried.

'To begin with, I knew you'd worry yourself sick over telling Darren about our engagement. I saw that day at the flat when he arrived unexpectedly to find us together that he resented me. I knew he'd regard me as a big bad wolf among the lambs, so I invited him here for the party to meet brother Jocelyn.'

'But what has Jocelyn to do with it? Darren hardly knows him.'

'Jocelyn is a surgeon and Darren is hoping to become a doctor. Naturally Darren will be interested in having a surgeon in the family.' There was laughter in the grey eyes as they held her green ones captive, laughter bordering on the old mockery. 'Darling, don't you know we begin from here?'

Reaching into the breast pocket of his jacket, he drew out a tiny box. The next moment the ring was on her engagement finger.

Davina gasped at the cluster of diamonds surrounding her birthstone.

'An emerald the colour of your eyes,' he whispered into her hair.

She shone up at him. 'But how did you know my size, and my birthstone? Don't tell me—Cheryl?'

His arms closed around her, and as his mouth claimed hers Davina knew that her future revolved around Nick; that for good or ill his arms were her world and she would never want it any other way.

The party was an enormous success. How could it not have been, Davina asked herself, with Nick taking charge. His personality filled the room. Everybody loved him, thought Davina, except Darren. She saw her brother after the speeches and the handing round of the cake ordered specially by Nick.

Darren looked brighter, but Davina knew that he was not entirely on her side.

'I'll be coming home one of these weekends,' he promised.

'Sorry you came?' she asked anxiously.

'No. At least I'm in for medicine, and do you know what? Nick's brother is going to get me into a special training hospital if I win my degrees. He's really interested in me.'

Davina hugged him. 'Nick will be pleased to have helped you. I meant what I said about keeping everything in the family. I'll be looking forward to seeing you as soon as you can make it.'

Nick drove Darren to the night express on his way to the flat to drop Davina off. Walking with her to the door, he opened it for her and went in with her to see if everything was all right. Cheryl and Rex had not returned.

Davina saw him to the door. With his arms around her he looked down hungrily into her face.

'How I hate this having to say goodnight to you instead of us spending our nights together,' he groaned against her lips. 'Our marriage can't come soon enough for me.'

Davina laughed on breath regained. 'You aren't trying to put through one of your international deals, darling, and we haven't got to get married, as it were.'

'I wouldn't swear to that,' he said darkly. 'The longer we remain apart the more we're tempting providence.'

CHAPTER SIX

THE next weekend that Darren came home was one when Davina was out for the day with Nick. Cheryl was at home because Rex was in Paris for the weekend selling a picture.

Davina had accompanied Nick to see a client who wanted a loan to buy a mansion in the country. The drive down to it took all of two hours through the most beautiful country.

The days were warming up to early summer weather and Davina had been asked to take her swimsuit. Nick was describing the house as he drove on the fast lane of the motorway.

'I'd like a place on similar lines. Nice and roomy for a family.'

'How much of a family? A football team?' she teased.

'As many as you like. I'm not fussy. I would like at least two,' he said, and she heard the smile in his voice. 'You like children, don't you, my sweet?'

'Love them,' she answered. 'Are you planning on giving these people the loan?'

'I'm reserving my judgment until I've seen through the place. I've had good reports as to the condition of the house and I believe the gardens have been kept in a good state of repair. However, there are lots of things to be taken into consideration and we can't afford to make mistakes.'

The grounds surrounding Hibernia House were

indeed very impressive, the lawns of green velvet
lending an elegant aura to the square mellowed
stone building. Over the stone walls and the per-
golas spanning the paths masses of flowers of every
hue cascaded down in glorious profusion.

Davina murmured, 'There has to be paddocks for
horses in a place like this.'

Nick said sardonically, 'This job is not really in
my line, but the loan required is a large one. Though
this man Smith appears to be genuine.'

'You have doubts?'

'Sort of.'

Mrs Smith greeted them on arrival. She was a
very attractive person with auburn hair and deep
brown eyes, a tall, slender girl with a gorgeous figure
who could not have been more than twenty or so.

'Thanks for coming,' she said as Nick introduced
Davina. 'It's fun being in the country, but my poor
Jay is wondering if it will be too quiet for me.'

James Smith joined them, a man in his sixties
who gave the impression that he had a grown-up
family tucked away somewhere in his past.

'Lovely figure, Mrs Smith,' Davina whispered in
an aside to Nick.

'No nicer than yours, my sweet,' Nick replied.

They were the only two guests for Sunday lunch,
which passed off very pleasantly. The Smiths had
been lucky to procure the services of an elderly
couple as resident housekeepers. The meal was ex-
cellently prepared and served.

There were to be more guests after lunch and it
proved to be a happy informal day. Nick had time
to make a detailed tour of the house before the
guests arrived.

There were about twenty guests in all ranging from young couples in their twenties to couples nearing middle age. The sun was out in force and most of them had come prepared to enjoy the afternoon at the marble outdoor swimming pool in the grounds.

A building containing cubicles where they could undress was nearby and Davina, in her brief swimsuit, found herself watching Nick as he strode towards her. He moved with an easy grace and she was aware of the rippling muscles beneath a skin of bronze satin, the thick cap of fair curls gleaming in the sun.

Placing a long careless arm around her slim shoulders, he said teasingly, 'Water too cold for you, my sweet?'

'I was waiting for you. Race you to the other end of the pool!'

He won although he had given her a start. Following her from the water, he slid his hands up the sides of her figure to cup her small firm bust warmly.

Davina leapt the rest of the stone steps to the side of the pool as if jet-propelled, making for the bath towel she had dropped before entering the water.

His smile was a pleasant taunt. 'Most girls with a figure like yours would be showing it off, not hiding it.'

Defensively, she cried, 'I'm not hiding it! I feel more comfortable in the towel.'

She met the provoking glint in his grey gaze. Her own eyes were wide, very green, her skin glowed like a sunwarmed peach.

'Because of me, you mean? I know what you're thinking. Or do I? You don't have to run away from me. You're perfectly safe.'

He pulled out a canvas chair by a small table on the side of the pool, seated her and slid on to the opposite chair.

Mrs Smith came to offer them an iced drink. She wore a brief swimsuit that revealed a perfect figure. Nick had an iced beer and Davina an iced Martini.

'Cheers!' Nick held up his glass and Davina touched it with hers.

'I'm sorry, Nick,' she said after a welcome drink. 'I know we're engaged, but ...'

'You can't bear me to touch you?' His smile was one of exasperation. 'What do you expect me to do —treat you like a sister?'

Davina laughed. 'Of course I don't. I can see that our engagement is going to be tempestuous and decidedly dangerous. I'll have to be on my toes.'

'I could tell you something that would be much more exciting and wonderful. Our marriage. Why don't we get married?' His eyes glinted as though at some private thought. 'You don't know what you're missing.'

'It's something to look forward to.' Davina lowered her eyes at the expression in his. It was going to be very hard to resist him. She loved him so much. Had she set herself an impossible task?

Upon arriving back at the flat Davina found Darren about to go to bed in order to catch an early train back to medical school.

'Sorry I missed you, Darren,' she said.

'You look all starry-eyed and kissed,' he said, and went to his room.

Cheryl smiled, 'Take no notice of him. He's jealous because someone else has your affection. He missed you when he arrived, but I made a nice dinner and he's enjoyed himself sunbathing on the roof all afternoon. I wouldn't be surprised if he isn't up half the night unable to sleep because of sunburn.'

She was right. Davina, going in his room before she went to bed, found him tossing and turning with no top bedcover and wearing only his pyjama trousers. His back was an angry red where the sun had scorched it.

Tenderly Davina smoothed calomine over the sore skin.

Lying on his stomach, Darren squinted up at her. 'I'm sorry I was so rude,' he said. 'But I was disappointed to find you out for the day.'

She felt guilty, and rather selfish. 'I understand. If I'd known you were coming I wouldn't have gone out.'

Later, lying in bed, Davina thought of Nick in an agony of longing and frustration that brought tears to her eyes. She was not too troubled to appreciate Darren's hurt and disappointment, but what was she to do? Torn between giving her brother some measure of security in his home life and wanting Nick with his mouth upon hers, the first a sense of duty and love, the second a fierce desire that cried out to be assuaged.

Nick called for her the following Thursday. In between he had sent her chocolates, candies, flowers, and paperbacks which he thought would interest her. The latter were crime stories written by a new woman author, but every time Davina tried to read one Nick's face would come between her and the printed page.

Davina looked at him hungrily as he strode towards her wearing his brilliant delighted smile. His embrace was enchanting, his face cool with a ruddy bronze laid on by endless trips abroad, his lips on hers warm and eager.

'Miss me?' he asked, and her heart wept bitter tears.

They drove out into the country for lunch. They were at the coffee stage when Davina said, 'About the loan for the Smiths' house? Did they get it?'

He was wearing a light grey summer weight suit with an arrogance that made everything he wore appear correct. He was willing her to look at him across the table in a way which shut out the rest of the world so that nothing else existed but a relentless magnetism that drew her eyes to his.

'I'm considering it,' he admitted at last. 'I have to go back to the city when we've finished lunch. There are one or two important calls coming for me from abroad and I have to be there.'

Davina quashed a sense of deep disappointment, not that there was not plenty to do at the flower shop even if it was half day closing.

'You're coming with me, of course,' he stated rather than asked.

'Oh!' Her surprised look gave way to a flickering smile. 'Where exactly are we going?'

'To my flat. Where else?' His grin teased. 'Afraid?'

'Why should I be?'

He said mockingly, 'Why should you be? Maybe I'm the one who should worry in case I'm not strong enough to resist you.' He paused, aware of her tenseness, and added tersely, 'Forget it. Let's go.'

On the way back he drove along a little used side

road to stop the car in a layby with full view of the fields beyond. He had let down the car windows to allow the sweet summer air in.

Davina lifted her head, taking in deep satisfying breaths of it.

Dreamily, she murmured, 'The summer is beautiful, isn't it. So miraculous how everything springs back into life after even an extra cruel winter.'

'Keep quiet and look,' he whispered. 'Over there at the far end of the field. See them?'

Davina followed his gaze to see two rabbits appear and playfully start to box each other. A tiny black one with a white powder puff tail took a ringside seat.

Davina giggled. 'Aren't they delicious? I don't know how anyone can shoot them.'

He placed an arm around her shoulders. 'Hares,' he said. 'I saw them the other day when I was up this way. I sometimes come to places like this for the peace and quiet I need sometimes in making certain decisions.'

'You mean you came to meditate about us, you and me?'

'Among other things. I was thinking that a wife could help.'

She was aware of his arm around her, sending wild vibrations through 'her body. She had to be strong.

On the edge of laughter, she cried, 'That's a tall story. Nick Tabor is sufficient unto himself. You wouldn't let a wife into your business life. Why, you won't even tell me what you've decided for the Smiths. You know very well what you're going to do about them.'

'Clever girl,' he whispered as he bent his head.

His mouth found hers casually, experimentally, and lingered no more than a second. Gradually his arms tightened and when he kissed her again the pounding of her blood made her panic.

'Didn't you say something about a telephone call?' she gasped on breath regained.

Nick's expression remained inscrutable. He was puzzled by her behaviour, she could tell. Nevertheless, he started the car and drove towards the city. His flat was in a quiet square shaded by trees, four-storied town houses converted into professional establishments for doctors, lawyers, writers and bankers and so on.

The wide oak front door had a highly polished knocker and shining letterbox. His flat was on the second floor. Inside he drew her along a corridor to a room at the end.

'The bathroom where you can freshen up,' he said into the curve of her neck at the back.

Davina turned swiftly in his arms. 'Thank you, darling, for showing me the rabbits. I loved them.'

'Hares,' he said laconically.

Her arms slid around his neck and when he released her he spoke unevenly.

'What I said about needing a wife is now beautifully illustrated by the clinch between us. I can now go to make my telephone calls with the happy anticipation of something to look forward to ... later,' he said darkly.

Davina slid from his arms. 'Nick?' she asked thoughtfully. 'Are we here alone?'

His chuckle was deep and tantalising. 'Afraid?' He made a playful feint beneath her chin. 'Now I have you guessing.'

She looked around at the deep pile carpet, the immaculate panelled walls, the well polished wide doors leading to the rooms in the corridor, the lovely flower arrangement in a window at the far end. A woman's touch if ever she saw one.

'A housekeeper?' she asked.

'A couple named Flowers in the basement.'

'Flowers?' Davina choked on the word, laughing quietly and helplessly.

'Awful, isn't it? I'm knee deep in them. Thank goodness you'll be giving up the shop when we're married.'

'But, Nick ...'

'See you later. I think I can hear the telephone in my study. The lounge is two doors down the corridor from the front door.'

He strode along the corridor to open a door and disappear inside leaving Davina staring after him helplessly.

The bathroom, in pale blue, sparkled with chrome fittings and well polished mirrors. Davina plunged her face in cold water and patted it dry, meeting wide troubled eyes in the mirror over the wash basin as she did so.

In the lounge she walked slowly to look out over the square where birds were flitting joyfully among the trees. So Nick expected her to give up the shop just as he would expect her to do anything else that he decreed. That was what he thought. He was in for a surprise if he thought he would have a docile wife.

For a while she wandered round the lounge admiring the deep easy chairs, the well chosen pieces of good furniture, the prints and etchings tastefully displayed on the walls. She sat down for a while, picked up the *Financial Times* from a low table nearby and flicked through it.

Nick's voice awakened her. He was standing over her with a cup of tea.

'Tea time,' he said with a smile. 'Mrs Flowers left everything ready. All I had to do was make the tea. Cake?'

He gave her a plate, then offered a sliced home-made plum cake. Davina took a small slice and watched him sit down in a comfortable chair nearby.

'Enjoy your sleep?' he enquired politely.

'Sleep? Have I been asleep?' Davina consulted her wrist watch. 'Gracious—five o'clock! What must you think of me? I'm the one who ought to have made the tea. Have you completed your business?'

He smiled, a charming smile that was one of his attractions and, to Davina's way of thinking, a most infuriating attribute at times.

Still under the impress of her sleep, she sat sipping the welcome tea, her eyes very green as she studied him.

'Almost,' he admitted. 'One more telephone call that didn't come through.'

She raised a delicate brow and he watched with pleasure the way her eyes with their tantalising tilt danced.

'A woman?' she queried.

'As a matter of fact it is, a real matriarch of a woman with a business head on her shoulders.'

'I take it you don't like career women?'

'No time for them. They're apt to become bossy and that is death to any marriage where the man is concerned.'

'Is that why you want me to give up working at
the flower shop?'

Nick raised a brow and reached to pour himself
another cup of tea. Then he leaned over to refill hers.

'I thought that was a foregone conclusion. Marriage is a full-time job, at least being married to me
will be.'

'But we haven't a house or anything yet!'

'We can look around for one. In fact, I have one
or two in mind.'

She said indignantly, 'You never said anything to
me about it.'

'I wanted to surprise you.'

'Fibber! You were going to buy one and take me
to see it, saying, "This is the house. Like it?" Well,
I won't be treated like that. Marriage is a partner-
ship between two people. You bought me this ring
instead of taking me with you to choose it myself.'

'I thought you liked it.'

'I do, but it isn't the same.'

He met her anger with an unruffled air. His com-
placency was proof against criticism from her or, indeed, from anyone.

He merely said, 'Take it back. I'll come with you
to choose another.'

She glared at him in exasperation. 'Oh, you make
me so mad! I could kill you!'

He eyed her with approval, taking in the tailored
dress of finely pleated green cotton that enhanced
the angry green sparkle of her eyes before he con-
centrated on her mouth.

His mouth quirked at the corners. 'Come and kiss
me instead,' he said wickedly.

'You're incorrigible, Nick Tabor, and I think it's

time I went home. I've kept you from your work long enough.'

Davina drank the rest of her tea, put down her cup and stood up. She moved forward to stand before him and he put down his cup to eye her lazily.

'What's the hurry?'

Before she knew what was happening he had her in his arms across his knees. She was like a bird caught in a snare, for he had her firmly pinned down with her legs over the arm of his chair.

Then he bent his head and claimed her lips. Davina closed her eyes and her heart was like a jumping bean. She resisted him as long as she could until the old magic began to work. As she relaxed in his arms his lips became more gentle and his hand moved over her back.

When he eventually released her Davina felt bruised and battered, with no breath for words and a nameless fear in her mind. Nick was the kind of man one would feel safer married to. She put an unsteady hand to her ruffled hair and he caught hold of it to kiss it.

There was laughter in his voice. 'And to think that I regarded you as being all gentle and dewy-eyed! I find this new Davina most stimulating.'

'Look, Nick,' she entreated, 'just let me go. It's so ridiculous being here in your arms and fighting.'

'I'm not fighting, my sweet, and don't you think you ought to stop behaving as if I was a big bad wolf instead of your intended?'

'It's all your fault.' She dug her fingers into the tight curls on his head. 'I've always wanted to do this,' she said.

'And do you want to live with me? Have you

given any thought to it?'

She said tentatively, 'Yes, I have. I don't want to be rushed, that's all. We have plenty of time.'

Nervously she pushed her fingers through the fair curls and he lifted a determined hand to grasp her wrist.

'Now relax,' he said brusquely, 'and tell me what's troubling you. Do you love me?'

Davina moved restlessly, as much as she could in his firm hold.

'Don't spoil our day, darling. I've been enjoying it up to now, please.'

She put her cheek against his hard unyielding one.

He said coldly, 'We aren't discussing a day in our lives, we're discussing all the years in the future. Either you want to marry me or you don't, and you haven't answered my question.'

'Oh, Nick! How can you ask such a question? Of course I love you. I'm crazy about you, but ...'

'But what?'

Davina swallowed on a dry throat. All free will seemed to have vanished. He was so agonisingly near. His fingers, strong as steel, were resting with deceptive lightness on her slender wrist. His other arm was clamped round her.

'Well? I'm waiting, Davina.'

She lifted her head but refused to meet his relentless gaze, looking down instead at the brown hand holding her wrist.

Haltingly she began, 'I'm not like you, free to do what you want to do. I have my family to think about. We're only just remaking our lives since my parents died. In a year or so ...'

'A year or so? What the devil are you talking about? If it's money you're bothered about I have plenty of it to pay for your brother's training or to set Cheryl up in anything she wants.'

'But don't you see, Nick? In about two years we shall really be getting somewhere with the shop and with the investments we've made.'

He laughed, a deep musical laugh that weakened her defences.

'Peanuts,' he scoffed, 'compared with what I can give you.'

'That's just it. Oh, I can't explain. You simply wouldn't understand,' she cried helplessly.

'Try me.'

She wriggled her wrist from his grasp and clasped his hand as if clinging to a lifeline. But if she was looking for help from him it was not there. He was frowning at her, a hint of anger bringing all the obstinate arrogance back to his face.

Davina tightened up inwardly. This was the Nick she was afraid of, who would ride along to brush anything fiercely away that stood in his path.

'Go on,' he urged inexorably. 'What else can you think up as an obstacle to our marriage?'

His grey eyes were as cold as the snows. Hers were wide green pools of distress.

She moistened dry lips. 'First I want to say that I love you very much and it would be wrong to let you think otherwise.'

'That's something anyway.' His manner changed, grew more gentle as he reached up to draw her head against his chest. 'Go on.'

'There's no problem with Cheryl apart from the fact that I want to stay with her in the shop until she has the hang of it. I do most of the paper work and go to the market for supplies and I have to land her with that gradually.'

'You could get a man to do all that,' he suggested. 'You need a man for the donkey work anyway.'

She sighed. 'We could hire a man now, but his pay would eat too much into our profits. Then there's Darren. He's still feeling lost after losing his home and his parents. Mother spoiled him and he will take a lot of diplomatic handling to keep him on an even keel. I ... I've tried to take my mother's place. You understand?'

'You little idiot! I understand perfectly. That's why I love you so much. You're sweetly honest, sincere and loving, and you care about others more than yourself. In fact you're a perfect fool when it comes to your own happiness. It doesn't grow on trees. You have to take it when it's offered.'

Nick fondled the brown cap of thick shining hair, his hand moving up from her waist to caress the curve of her cheek.

'Suppose you let me handle it? I've had a great deal of experience in handling all kinds of people.'

Davina quivered as she recalled Darren's dependence on her.

'I'll do it,' she answered, stubbornly insistent. 'I'll talk to Darren.'

There was a brief silence, then Nick dropped his hand to her waist.

'You know that you have to give me a date for our wedding if I agree to that, don't you? Say three weeks from now?'

'Three weeks? But isn't that a bit unreasonable? I ... I mean ... three weeks? Nick, you don't know what you're asking! It would be one mad rush.'

He smiled. 'A beautifully mad rush. Don't you agree?'

She gripped the hand still holding hers and clung to it. Love, she had discovered, was not a quiet feeling of love and contentment. It was a wild rushing stream which carried you along, swerving around rocks and boulders to the final fulfilment.

Nick had treated the family problems as unimportant in regard to their happiness. To his mind they could be filed away like any other problems he had dealt with. But Nick did not carry a mental picture of Darren cut adrift from an adoring mother, sent away from home when his main anchor had been taken up for ever. Desperately, she played for time.

'Six weeks,' she said.

He laughed and hugged her. 'You strike a hard bargain, my sweet. It's Darren, isn't it?'

'But how did you know what I was thinking?'

'Because you and I belong together. Between us we make a whole—a rare thing to happen between people. We're going to be content with each other for the rest of our lives!'

Nick looked at his watch. 'My telephone call is due. When I've taken it we shall go to the kitchen to see about our dinner. Mrs Flowers has left everything to hand. I hope you don't mind a cold banquet?'

'Anything with you is nectar,' she said.

He had to show her then in actions that he appreciated her compliment. He was going to his study for the telephone call when she said, 'What's the name of your lady client?'

His eyes gleamed wickedly. 'That, my sweet, is something I can't divulge to you. My business is private and secrecy is vital. I'm fairly ruthless where my work is concerned. Be with you in five minutes.'

That evening was one of the happiest Davina had ever spent. There was much laughter and fooling in the kitchen with Nick knowing where everything was kept and knowing something about cooking as well. It was he who made the coffee and carried everything in to the dining room.

'You're not marrying a helpless nitwit, darling. I can look after you and myself too.'

Davina nodded happily, finding it hard to believe that the whole stupid worry about her family was already on the way to being solved. The important thing to do was to keep on the shop for a while after they were married, working for the same end that she had visualised from the start of her business venture.

At her door as he was kissing her goodnight, she sighed.

'See you next Thursday, darling.'

He raised a fair brow. 'You're seeing me tomorrow evening—or should I say late afternoon, before the shops close. I'm taking you to pick your own engagement ring.'

Her blankness gave way to a surprised look. 'But I already have one. Remember?'

He kissed the ring. 'You can keep it for a dress ring. You're going to have one you have chosen yourself.'

'Oh, but, Nick—I don't want another. This is fine. I love it.'

'All the same, you're going to have one of your

own choice,' he told her firmly. 'You can leave the shop an hour or so before closing and leave Cheryl to cope.'

'But I can't,' she wailed. 'Friday is one of our busiest days.'

He regarded her with a half smile. 'The whole day on Monday, then. We can combine all our shopping then in one day.'

Davina looked at him blankly. 'All our shopping?'

His eyes twinkled wickedly. 'That's right. We have only six weeks. Remember?'

Davina's green eyes widened as she comprehended. With a youthful dignity which made his mouth quirk with amusement, she said primly, 'Nick Tabor, if you think I'm going to allow you to buy my trousseau you have another think coming! I'd never dream of such a thing. My mother would turn in her grave!'

He put his face close to her warm one. 'And so she would too if you insist upon torturing me by your indecision. I'm going to make sure you have no excuses about not being ready when the time comes. So go and have your beauty sleep. See you on Monday at ten sharp.'

CHAPTER SEVEN

THAT weekend was the busiest Davina and Cheryl had ever had to cope with. They were run off their feet. Consequently, Davina had little time to talk to her sister about the plans for an early marriage. Then Nick telephoned on Saturday morning from Brussels to change their shopping day on the following Monday to Tuesday. He had had to go away unexpectedly. Davina felt as if she had been granted a reprieve from she knew not what.

Juleen called at the shop on Saturday afternoon to order flowers. She was accompanied by a tall, statuesque young woman who appeared to be very interested in the shop.

Her hair was a pale gold and combed in a loose knot at the back of her head. Her eyes were a cool pale blue. She wore a very smart mushroom-coloured silk suit set off by a matching cape. An elegant creature of enigmatic expression, thought Davina, Swedish probably and not much older than herself.

Juleen introduced Davina as Nick's fiancée and her friend as Birgit Akland. While Davina attended to Juleen, Birgit wandered around the shop picking up flower baskets and plant pots with long, enamelled, pink-tipped fingers. She made several purchases of elegant flower holders and pretty decorated plant pots to be sent to Juleen's place.

'Who do you think she is?' asked Cheryl. 'A film star?'

'I don't think so.' Davina carried on with her task of packing the stuff they had ordered. 'She wore no ring, so I would guess that her father is a rich tycoon or something.'

Cheryl walked around the shop like a model with her hand on her hip.

'Do you think a cape would suit me?' Suddenly she swung round to gaze at her sister. 'You could dress like that if you married Nick,' she said.

Davina placed fern with a spray of tulips and said very quietly, 'I will, in six weeks' time.'

Cheryl gave a gasp. 'You're not! I don't believe it. You can't be—you're too calm about it.'

'That's what you think.'

'How long have you known?'

'Since Thursday night. I've been wondering how to tell you.'

'Since Thursday night?' Cheryl's voice rose in her excitement. 'And you never said until now. You dark horse! Aren't you absolutely thrilled about it?'

Davina gave a nervous laugh. 'I don't think it's registered yet, quite frankly. Do you mind?'

'Mind? I'm over the moon about it! We must celebrate. Have you written to Darren?'

'Of course not. I wanted to tell you first. Besides, I have to tell Darren personally. I don't know how he's going to take it.'

'Don't worry about it. He'll get over it,' Cheryl gave a delighted cry. 'Whoopee! We must celebrate. Where shall we go?'

Davina said, 'There's really nothing to celebrate —after all, we are engaged. We can have a special little dinner at the flat, but I have to put things right with Darren first. We don't know how he's going to react. I do hope he takes it the right way.'

Cheryl smiled brightly. 'We can ask him to come this weekend.'

Davina frowned. 'I don't want to take him away from his studies, but I have to tell him soon.'

Later Davina delivered the last of the week's orders, leaving Belcourt Mansions until the last. At Juleen's door she paused, wondering if Nick had told his sister-in-law of his forthcoming marriage, and decided to say nothing.

Birgit opened the door and asked her in. 'Juleen wants to see you,' she said with a cool smile. 'She will be with you in a moment.'

Davina put down the flowers, then went out to fetch the rest of the order. When she returned Birgit had left the room and Juleen came forward tying a wrap hastily.

'I was taking a bath,' she explained. 'Do sit down. Would you like a sherry? You look tired.'

Davina shook her head, pushing the heavy hair from her aching forehead. It was not the pressure of work causing the pain, it was the thought of Darren. He had to come first whatever reaction he had to her marriage.

She smiled brightly. 'Nothing to drink, thanks. We've had a particularly busy weekend, run off our feet.' She sighed. 'I'm going home to put them up.'

She sat down gratefully as Juleen perched on the arm of a nearby chair.

Folding slender hands displaying several rings, Juleen said, 'I don't suppose you know where Nick is? No one seems to know, not even his secretary. As his fiancée you should know something of his whereabouts.'

Davina shook her head. 'I can only tell you he's somewhere abroad and he'll be back for Tuesday. We have a date then.'

'I see.' Juleen studied beautifully manicured nails and appeared to make up her mind about something, for she frowned before going on, 'Birgit is anxious to see him as soon as possible. Business, you understand?' Another pause, then, 'I don't suppose it will mean anything to you as you're engaged and will be giving up the shop anyway.'

Davina's aching feet were forgotten and a trickle of a chill ran down her spine. She moistened her dry lips.

'Is there something I ought to know?' she asked.

Juleen shrugged slim shoulders. 'Maybe you already know. Rumours do get around, and you've probably heard that your flower shop is part of a block being sought after by several concerns, including a Swedish one of which Birgit is the head.'

Davina drew in a breath that hurt her lungs. 'So that's why she took such an interest in the shop when she came in with you? And Nick never told me!'

The colour left her face as she took it in. What hurt more at the moment was Nick not saying anything to her about it. She remembered what he had said about being ruthless in his job regarding absolute secrecy, but this time it concerned her.

Her green eyes were dull with disillusionment and pain.

'Am I right in thinking that Birgit is seeking a loan from Nick in order to buy the block?' she enquired dully.

Juleen moved uncomfortably. 'I'm sorry if I've let the cat out of the bag, so to speak, but I really thought you knew. You see, this deal has been going on for all of six months.'

Davina's face went ashen. Six months? Before Nick had made himself known to them. So that was the reason he had cold-shouldered the bigger flower shops in the town in favour of theirs. He had to find out how the land lay, even to the point of getting engaged to herself. But surely that was going too far in the matter of his job?

Driving back to the flat she kept asking herself—why? Not that she was foolish enough to suppose that Nick had committed himself to marriage against his will in order to further a deal.

Perhaps if she had fallen into his arms as he had expected her to do in the first place he would have not hesitated to tell her about the shop being taken over.

Davina was tired after a gruelling week and her brain felt woolly. She had worked hard night and day to work up a business and had been proud of its success. Now it was all to go down the drain, like her plans to increase their money in the bank.

Cheryl had gone out for the evening with Rex and she arrived home to an empty flat too weary to make herself a cup of tea after putting the van away. She sank down on the settee and put her feet up, too exhausted in mind and body to think straight. Her eyes closed.

When she awoke it was morning. Someone had taken off her shoes and covered her with an eider-down; Cheryl, who would be sleeping in as she usually did on Sunday morning.

Surprisingly Davina had slept well, but she felt too restless to relax. Putting on the kettle for a cup of tea, she telephoned her accountant, an old friend of her father's. He told her that he had heard rumours that the block including the flower shop was on the market, but nothing specific. It could be that it had been kept quiet because the Swedish company were after it. He also congratulated her on her engagement and he was sure Nick Tabor would be able to help her concerning the shop being up for sale.

Davina put down the telephone with some misgiving. The engagement had evidently been reported in the newspapers, of which she saw very little. Had Darren seen it? She shrugged mentally. What did it matter? The engagement was off now in any case.

The day passed uneventfully with Davina deciding about telling Cheryl about the possible closing of the shop. Time to tell her when she had found out more from Nick.

Monday was a quiet day at the shop and they did some spring-cleaning and stocktaking. That evening Cheryl invited Rex to dinner and Davina went to visit an old friend. She stayed for tea and on her way home telephoned Nick's apartment from a phone booth.

Mrs Flowers, the housekeeper, answered the telephone to say that he was expected back that evening. She was there preparing him a late meal. Yes, it was all right if Davina came round. She would leave the door unlocked for her to go in as she was on the point of leaving for her own quarters.

Davina let herself into the apartment to meet silence. Walking to the lounge, she took off her coat and sat on the settee. The task in front of her was something she shrank from. Yet it had to be done.

Leaning back against the cushions, she wondered at Nick's reaction on discovering her knowledge of a transaction he had kept from her.

When the shrill ringing of the telephone nearby rent the air she reached out an arm to pick up the receiver, fully expecting to hear Nick's voice.

But it was Birgit enquiring if he had returned home. Davina replied that he had not and put down the receiver without revealing her identity. The woman apparently meant business.

Nick came around eight o'clock, striding into the flat and pausing at the hall table to pick up his mail. She wanted to run out to meet him, to feel his cool mouth on her own sending all kinds of delicious tremors through her; she wanted him so much that tears smarted in her eyes like sand.

Long afterwards she remembered the beating of her heart sending flutterings in her throat like moths' wings as he walked into the room. He was sorting through his letters and he lifted his head slowly as if alerted to a presence in the room. His brows slowly lifted and his mouth curved into a devastating smile.

'Darling!' he exclaimed. 'Why didn't you let me know what a treat I had in store for me? Let me look at you.'

He dropped the letters on to a small table and strode forward to take her in his arms. Apart from standing up Davina made no move. She felt his hands grip her arms as he smiled down into her face.

'No kiss?' he asked wryly.

'I want to talk to you,' she answered, holding herself rigid.

'And I want to kiss you and hold you for ever.'

He did kiss her and very thoroughly until it seemed to Davina that he was going to hold her for ever. Her heart was a crazy thing entirely out of her control and all she could do was to cling until he let her go.

The smile on his face had gone and he eyed her with a curious look.

'Is anything wrong?' he asked. 'You look frightfully pale. I'm a brute, aren't I? But I've been away from you so long. I suppose you're dead beat after a day at the shop? I'll get you a drink.'

Davina was beyond words and sat down as he poured out drinks for them both.

'Here you are, darling. Cheers.'

She took the drink mechanically, murmuring her thanks and hoping that it would give her the courage she needed.

Nick sipped his drink, still standing to look down on her.

'Still shattered, darling?' he teased. 'But you can't say I took you by surprise when you were waiting for my arrival.'

'No, I can't, can I?' she said shakily.

Why did she not talk? Whatever doubt had held her back had been breached by his teasing. There was no time for her to say anything before the telephone rang.

Nick put down his glass and took the call. He spoke for seconds briefly and concisely.

'Yes . . . I understand . . . yes. Shall we say Wednesday? See you then.'

'Birgit?' asked Davina.

He put down the telephone and raised a brow.

'How did you know?'

She said quietly, 'Why didn't you tell me about the shop and the surrounding block being on the market?'

He shrugged. 'Because you'll soon be out of it anyway.'

'How do you know?' she cried indignantly. 'How do you know that I might have wanted Cheryl to carry on?'

'But you wouldn't, would you? You told me yourself that you did all the accounts and the buying in. Cheryl would never do all that on her own.'

'Is that why you came to our shop in the first place, to look around?'

Nick shoved his hands into his pockets and frowned down at her.

'You are feeling sore aren't you, darling, just because I didn't take you into my confidence. I told you I was ruthless where my work is concerned?'

'You can say that again,' she cried indignantly. 'Spying on us and pretending to be a customer!'

'Spying on you? What rubbish you're talking. Why should I spy on you?'

'Well, weren't you? You had to see that everything was on your side regarding a loan towards purchasing the property.'

He said coldly, 'I'm not a house agent nor a representative of a building society. I'm an international banker and the purchase of your shop has nothing to do with me.'

'Then why is this Birgit person staying with your sister-in-law? And why is she telephoning you? She made a call here once before tonight while I was here.'

'Why didn't you ask her?'

'Because it's none of my business.'

'Exactly.'

'Oh, dear! What am I saying?' Davina raised her hands to burning cheeks. 'Of course it's my business if the shop is on the market.'

'For the love of Mike,' he exclaimed harshly, 'do you actually think I came to your shop and made advances to you simply to get the business for a client?' His laugh was devoid of humour. 'I'd hardly propose to you for a paltry thing like that. Surely you know I'm not that kind of person?'

Davina teetered between throwing herself into his arms and standing her ground.

'But why didn't you tell me about the shop?'

'I didn't know about it. Besides, it has to go.'

She flicked an angry finger. 'Just like that?'

'Why make a song about it? You're making it too important,' he said firmly. 'You know very well you couldn't possibly carry on with the shop when once we are married. We shall be looking around for a house.'

'But if we live in your flat in the meantime I shall have heaps of time to go to the flower shop. Look at the times you have to go abroad when I shall be left on my own.'

'So you had it all worked out. You were going to go working in the shop on a long engagement. My setting the date of our marriage brought you down to earth.'

'You seem to forget that we haven't known each other five minutes.'

Nick said bluntly, 'I knew within the first few seconds of seeing you that I loved you. It's plain to see that you didn't feel the same. I can see now that by proposing an early marriage I was destroying the cosy little world you'd created. You imagined us going on for a year or so being engaged.'

Davina twisted her hands. 'What if I did? Is it any worse than you demanding that we marry right away? The trouble with you is you want everything your way!'

'That makes two of us.' His eyes hardened. 'What do you want, some weak idiot who'll bow to all your wishes? Heaven knows why you thought I would stand for any of your nonsense.'

Her face was pale, her eyes dark with unhappiness. 'I explained why I wanted us to wait before getting married. But that isn't what we're quarrelling about, actually. It's this Birgit person who's determined to buy the shop. Juleen said negotiations have been going on for six months.'

His mouth thinned. 'And I told you I didn't know anything about it then. However, you seem to want to make me out a liar and several other things beside.' He was suddenly very angry. 'I wonder you dare trust yourself here alone with me in the flat, thinking what you do. Or is this a way of getting out of our marriage? Well, aren't you afraid?'

He hauled her into his arms. 'God, woman! Don't you know that I love you?' His arms were like steel closing in on her. 'Isn't it time you and I understood each other?'

Davina strained against his hold, but all to no avail. Then his lips were on hers. The world tilted as he spoke her name and she was conscious only of his strength and his kisses that were taking her very soul from her body. She held on as he whispered between kisses with a thickness in his voice.

'Darling Davina, you know you belong to me. You're mine now and for ever. You can't deny it.'

It was the sheer masculine arrogance in his words that stung her out of her stupor, deafened her to everything except the present. Everything was coming back to her, why she was here at the flat, all that he had done behind her back. And he had not explained Birgit.

He had manipulated her as he had his business associates. She was to be another of his easy conquests. But she would show him. She fought him blindly to free herself.

'Let me go!' she cried, striking him furiously, then recoiling at the red angry mark on his cheek where her fingers had been.

Her rage died as if blown out by an east wind. She shivered, suddenly ashamed of herself. There was only one thing for it. With trembling fingers she tore off her engagement ring and held it out to him.

Nick's eyes were grey steel as he ignored her action.

He said coldly, 'I'll take you home. You're over-tired and I am too.'

He strode to the door and held it open for her. For a moment she stood gazing at him, then dropping the ring on the low table beside his glass, she walked towards him.

The speed he set up as he drove back to her flat forced her to cling to her seat. Neither of them spoke, her brain reeled, with the slap she had given him echoing in her distraught mind. When Nick braked at her door Davina was out of the car in a trice. Then he had gone.

The flat was quiet when she opened the door with her key. She listened for several moments with bated breath before making her way to the kitchen. It was empty of Cheryl and Rex who were evidently in the lounge. Hastily searching for a scrap of paper and a pen, Davina scribbled a few words to the effect that she was feeling tired and had gone to bed.

But in her room that tiredness did not induce sleep. She lay for a long time going over the evening again and again. One thing she had learned was that she loved Nick whatever he had done. Their engagement was not over. He would telephone in the morning. They would go shopping and he would replace the ring on her finger.

As for Darren, she could talk to him, make him understand how important it was for her to marry the man she loved.

In her worried state Davina slept little that night and was hard put to it to rise at four-thirty in the morning in order to go to the Tuesday early morning market for her flowers.

Early morning market days were Tuesdays and Thursdays and it was unknown for the men at the market to see her without her usual sunny smile. This morning, though, Davina was finding it difficult to put on a bright face. She was teased about it and took it in good part.

Strange that it had not occurred to her until now how she would miss the friendly banter from the men of all ages who found her a doll. There had been no message for her from Nick, Cheryl told her on her arrival back at the shop. Davina had decided not to tell Cheryl about their quarrel, it was too painful at the moment even to think about.

By the afternoon it became almost certain that Nick had no intention of getting in touch with her. Slackly she went about her work in the shop, and around four o'clock Juleen came in.

She said, 'I was surprised you didn't lunch with us today. I know it's your market day, but I thought you would have managed it, seeing that Birgit was there.'

Davina felt her heart slip painfully. 'I don't know what you're talking about.'

Juleen was taken aback. 'But surely you said you and Nick had a date today? Or is it this evening? Come to think of it, when I remarked on your absence he pretended he didn't hear.'

'You mean Nick had lunch with you and Birgit?'

'My husband as well, of course.'

Davina said quietly, 'I know Nick was seeing Birgit on Wednesday—he arranged a meeting while I was there last evening in his flat early on. I had no idea he was seeing her today. Have you heard anything more of the sale of this shop?'

'No, but then Nick will keep you posted.' Juleen's eyes narrowed thoughtfully. 'Is there anything wrong between you and Nick? You seem a little odd.'

Cheryl looked up from putting some very pretty plant pots on display on a shelf and glanced curiously at her sister.

'Davina always looks tired after going to the early market,' she stated. 'Rather her than me. I'd hate to get up so early.'

'I shall have to use more make-up if it's so obvious,' Davina cut in, anxious to prevent Juleen from probing further. Juleen's remarks grated.

Whereas before she was always a welcome customer now her presence brought Nick intolerably near.

Juleen said sweetly, 'I should go out with Nick tomorrow when he sees Birgit if I were you. She's very much like him, in fact you could almost say she's the female equivalent of Nick—blonde, beautiful, and out to get what she wants regardless. I should be on my toes if I were you as long as she's in town.'

Davina moved a few blooms from an almost empty vase to a partly filled one and picked up the empty one to wash it out.

'Nick can't bear clever women. He told me so, even if they do have a very attractive accent.'

She was unprepared for Juleen's angry flush. Good heavens, she thought, Juleen really does think she's clever herself and has taken umbrage.

She smiled to take away the sting she had not intended.

'That's why he's so fond of me,' she said sweetly.

But Juleen was not amused. She said stiffly, 'I invited Nick to bring you to dinner this evening, but he wouldn't commit himself. What about you?'

Davina walked slowly to the beaded curtain with the vase. Her smile was disarming.

'You'd better leave it to Nick,' she said. 'I have no idea what he has in mind for tonight.'

Juleen had gone when Davina finally emerged into the shop after washing the vase.

'What was the matter with her?' Cheryl asked at the till. 'And what's this about the shop being for sale?'

'Just something I heard. I don't know any more than that. Do you think I bought enough tulips?'

Cheryl gave the flower display a cursory glance. She was not to be sidetracked.

'And didn't Juleen say something about you going out with Nick today?' she probed.

'Yes,' Davina answered reluctantly, not feeling up to discussing him. 'You know how Nick is. He has these important unexpected assignments.'

'And he must meet a lot of women in the length of the day.'

Davina laughed. 'And what's that supposed to mean?'

'Only that Juleen could be right. You ought to grab the man while you can.'

Davina almost said she was already engaged, then remembered that she was not. And Nick had not made any attempt to get in touch with her. Come to think of it, perhaps everything had happened for the best and she was better remaining her own mistress doing her own thing.

Darren would be happy, and Cheryl. In time she might even be happy herself. Since knowing Nick she had been on a kind of see-saw, first up, then down. Davina had almost convinced herself when the telephone rang just before five and Cheryl took the call.

'It's Nick,' she whispered urgently.

Davina's heart beat like a sledgehammer as she picked up the phone.

'Davina?' The deep voice ran along her nerves like a flash of lightning running along an electric cable. 'I came for you this morning as arranged to find that you weren't at the flat or the shop. I let it rest there thinking you would have cooled down

by now. Can we meet this evening, or shall I come
to the flat?'

'Neither,' she told him. 'Our engagement was a
mistake. I happened to be at the early morning
market and didn't return until after ten.'

'But you knew we were going out?'

'It was you who changed the day to Tuesday.'

'So it was.' A pause. 'And you did say our engagement was a mistake? Are you playing chicken?'

'No, I'm not.'

'But you can't leave it at that!' he protested. 'I'm
coming round now—we have to talk about it.'

'I'm sorry, I've no time—besides, I need an early
night. Goodbye, Nick.'

No time for him: that was it. But Davina's
thoughts were in a turmoil. She had made up her
mind she was going to forget him. She was never
going to think about him at all. She was trembling
as she put down the telephone. It was awful how the
decision hurt, made her feel so desolate. The bleak-
ness of the sudden ending to her engagement, the
finality of it, weighed heavily upon her. Cheryl did
not help things. Davina had never seen her so
shocked.

'You must be barmy to give a man like Nick up!
What got into you?'

To put herself on a more even keel, Davina asked,
'What time did you open the shop this morning?'

Cheryl went a dull red. 'Just before you came
from the market. You know I sleep like a log and I
rely upon you waking me.'

'Then Nick must have found the shop closed and
gone on to the flat and failed to make you hear.'

'I'm sorry,' Cheryl mumbled.

'It doesn't matter,' said Davina wearily. 'What will be will be. At least I don't have to explain to Darren about getting married.'

Cheryl said eagerly, 'If there's anything I can do like explaining to Nick, I'll do it willingly.'

'Let's leave it, shall we? How are you going on with Rex? You've been very quiet about him lately.'

'All right,' laconically.

Davina sighed inwardly. Aloud, she said, 'I'm going out with the orders, so if Nick calls you don't know where I am.'

CHAPTER EIGHT

DAVINA knew she would miss Nick, but she had never imagined how dreadful life would be without him. On the Wednesday at lunch time she had tortured herself imagining him having lunch with Birgit. He did not come to the shop or the flat again and she heard no more about him for a few days.

Then one day she ran into Juleen after delivering an order to Belcourt Mansions. Juleen was about to go in as she came out.

'Hello, Davina,' she smiled. 'What have you been doing with yourself? Now that Nick's away we should have got together, but I'm awfully busy at the moment.'

'So are we. Have you heard from Nick?'

'No. I suppose you have. How is he?' Juleen eyed her curiously as she asked the question, and Davina wondered if Nick had told her that they had split up.

She decided to play it slowly until she was sure because Nick was not the kind of person who would discuss his personal life with anyone.

'He's well as far as I know. How's your husband?'

'He's doing a series of lectures at local hospitals. We must have lunch together one day.'

'That would be nice.'

Davina smiled warmly, knowing that Juleen did not intend going further with the suggestion. For some reason or other Juleen had become distant and cool. At times, as now, she appeared almost as an enemy.

She said on parting, 'Did Nick tell you that he travelled to Sweden with Birgit? That man certainly does live it up! First class travel to far away places with glamorous companions thrown in.'

Davina went to her van like a sleepwalker. She had no reason to doubt the truth of what Juleen had said since the woman knew she could check later with Nick as to the truth of it. It was obvious to Davina that Nick had said nothing to Juleen or his brother about their broken engagement, which meant precisely nothing since Davina had no doubt about the break being final.

The week went by with no word from Nick. Davina wore herself out trying to find an antidote to her suffering in work. Her social life was nil. She had neither the heart for it nor the energy. Then one evening, Thursday, Juleen telephoned to ask her to come over for an hour or so. She was on her own and if they had nothing to talk about Davina could give her a lesson in flower arrangement.

Her first reaction was to refuse, but she recalled how kind Juleen had been to her in coming to the shop and recommending her to her friends. She had been at home most of the afternoon, since it was early closing day, doing the accounts, so it would be a welcome break. She put on a pale blue moth's wing of a dress in billowing chiffon with a cape effect top and trod into silver sandals with ankle straps.

Cheryl, who was staying in to wash her hair and read a new favourite paperback, gave a mock exclamation of surprise.

'You look lovely, my dear sister,' she cried. 'Your dress looks as if no mortal hand has touched it. What a pity it's to be wasted on someone like Juleen. Wear my evening shawl with it—the one Rex brought me from Paris. You'll look delicious.'

To Davina's surprise Juleen came in her car to collect her. Cheryl heard it stop below the lounge window in the street. She surveyed the car with a hint of amusement in her eyes.

'You're going to Belcourt Mansions in style,' she commented.

Davina felt somewhat diffident at meeting Juleen again, but there was no cause for apprehension. She gave Davina a warm smile and complimented her on her dress.

'You look beautiful, my dear, and all for me,' she said as Davina gathered up her skirts and slid into the car beside her. 'You weren't going anywhere, were you? I mean, I haven't put you out at all?'

Davina shook her head. 'No. I was free to come.'

As they went into the flat Juleen pushed Davina gently into the lounge.

'Won't be a moment. I left Jocelyn getting ready to go out. I must see if he's gone or if he has time to take a drink with us.'

Davina slipped off her shawl and went to sit down on the comfortable settee, smoothing her full skirt neatly under her. Leaning her head back, she sighed contentedly. In the quietness of the room she thought about Nick. What was the use of pretending she had hoped he would keep away from anywhere she was likely to go?

It was possible for her to bump into him any time. Any day in which she did not see him was empty, completely barren. To Davina it had seemed like years since she had last seen him, but there were many such years ahead. If she must be miserable how much better to be miserable seeing him than not to see him.

Juleen came back full of apologies for keeping Davina waiting. Jocelyn, her husband, was in tow.

'Sorry, Davina, to leave you like that. Jocelyn, pour the drinks.' Her smile at Davina was warm. 'This is the best part of the day for me, these quiet precious few moments when Jocelyn and I relax over a drink in the evening at the end of the day. Cheers!'

She lifted her glass to Davina as Jocelyn passed round the drinks before sitting down in a chair to face his wife and Davina on the settee.

He enquired about Darren and admitted that he was very impressed by the boy. While it was a little early to give a sound judgment on Darren's merits, he believed himself to be something of a psychologist and would say that he had a sound future in front of him.

Davina, of course, was delighted, and it made her evening when Jocelyn told her that he would help Darren in any way he could if he had any problems. Davina, listening to him, realised what a good father he would have made. He was not as attractive physically as Nick, but there was the same steadfastness of character. He was a man who had fought hard to get where he was but had fought cleanly, like Nick.

Nick! The very thought of him brought a lump

to her throat, for Jocelyn brought him back so clearly by the lift of a brow and the same deep chuckle.

'I'm afraid I must go,' said Jocelyn, glancing at his watch before finishing his drink.

Juleen was on her feet, giving him her empty glass to put down on the low table with his own.

'I'll come to see you off, dear,' she said with another apologetic smile at Davina. 'Don't you think, Jocelyn, you might fill Davina's glass?'

They were on the point of leaving the room when Juleen exclaimed, 'Nick! Just in time. You can entertain Davina while I'm gone.'

Nick's deep tones struck Davina's heart like a gong.

'Thanks for doing this for me,' he replied. 'I'm very grateful.'

'Not in the least.' Joceyln's voice this time. 'I hope we shall be seeing you again soon. We don't see half enough of you these days.'

'Not too soon, I'm sorry to say. I'm off again soon to Brussels for a few days. But I'll be back.'

'So you're not deserting us after all? I'm so glad.' Juleen tiptoed to kiss his tanned cheek. 'See you soon, Nick.'

Nick moved from the door to allow them to pass him, and conscious of him closing it and coming towards her, Davina, who had willed herself to keep cool, found her heart thudding loud enough for him to hear.

'Hello, Davina.' Nick was standing in front of her and as she looked up he bent to take the glass from her trembling hand. 'Here, let me take that before you spill it.'

'Now let me look at you.' He had put down the glass and had bent down once more to take her hands in his and pull her to her feet. As he gripped her small hands he saw the slightly tilted eyes widen and the pink colour rush beneath her clear skin.

'Well, darling? Aren't you pleased to see me?' he demanded audaciously with an endearing grin. 'It seems like years since we met and you have no right to look so desirable, and lovely. You should be pining away with love for me.'

But all Davina could do was to stare and go on staring at someone she had longed to see again with all her being. What chance had she against a delightful person who had charm, wit, good looks and the most enchanting voice in the world?

'Nick?' she whispered breathlessly. 'Oh, Nick!'

Those minutes in one's life that are spent in a delirium of bliss are always far too short. As that long kiss ended, Davina drew back to look up into his lean arrogant face.

How she loved him, and in her love she saw him for the first time through tender eyes. She saw the slightly anxious look behind the devilment in his grey eyes and knew that though he might have taken his fun where he found it, he had also collected quite a few hard knocks on the way.

If only she could have seen him like this at their first meeting! But the regret that it could not possibly have been so was added to another pain.

'You said you're going away again?'

'I have to, my darling. But I can't wait to get it over because then I have lots of leave coming to me——'

'Oh!' Davina was incapable of saying anything more. It was too heavenly to give in to his nearness and dearness. Later, when all the magic had dimmed, the whole unhappy situation would maybe torture her again. At this precious moment of time she could only think that tomorrow he might be gone.

He said, 'When I come back we're going to see Cheryl and Darren and tell them we're going to be married. Then they can tell us if they approve or not.'

She looked at him in amazement, shaken at his uncanny knack of striking at the heart of the situation.

'But what made you suggest that?' she asked.

'Because, my sweet, you'll discover how little it will matter to them. I have a great opinion of their common sense.'

'Nick!' she protested. 'I know Cheryl will be all for us marrying, but Darren is another matter. He'll see the real outcome of it.'

'And what's that? That he'll acquire an older brother who'll become a welcome buffer between him and two lovely sisters who adore him but who are smothering him with kindness.'

'But we're not!' she wailed. 'Which shows how little you understand the situation. Please, let's not talk about it now.'

'Very well.' Nick's arms tightened around her, and he bent his head. Ardent moments ticked by and when he raised his head, he said a little thickly, 'Let's go to my place. I want you all to myself and I have a meal all laid on.'

Breathlessly, she said, 'But what about Juleen? I

came to keep her company.'

She searched his face with wide eyes and saw the answer in his tender smile.

'You mean she lured me here in order to meet you?' she gasped.

She disengaged herself with a blank look of disbelief on her face.

'Don't look at me like that,' he said harshly. 'I had to do something to get you back.'

But her expression turned to one of horror. 'You mean Jocelyn and Juleen were in it with you, and all that Jocelyn said about my brother Darren was all spoken with you in mind? All that talk about Darren having a wonderful future and Jocelyn being his friend for life was engineered to put my mind at rest about marrying you?'

He caught her shoulders and Davina thought he was going to shake her.

'Stop saying things that aren't true!' he snapped angrily. 'And calm down. Why must you have to make an issue out of everything? Juleen and Jocelyn don't even know that we quarrelled. They think I engineered your visit here as a surprise after my being away. Come on, let's go to my place. My brother and his wife have gone out together.'

The rest of that evening passed as in a dream. The meal had been left ready for them and Davina helped Nick to bring in the dishes from the kitchen. Nick's flat with his identity stamped all over it as a bachelor's domain set up all kinds of vibrations inside her.

The lobster cocktail, cold chicken accompanied by a fresh salad, and a tall frosty bottle of Rhine wine and the bowl of fruit which followed left little room for the cheeses and biscuits which rounded off the meal.

Nick teased her during the meal about her heightened colour and saw that she ate a good meal, then they sat together on the settee for coffee which he made.

With his arm around her and her head against his chest they listened to records until it was quite late.

'I hate to see you go,' he groaned. 'The time I'm away will be like years. What shall I do without you?'

He kissed the glossy brown cap of hair, moved down to her mouth, then he was kissing the warm hollow of her throat. She pushed her fingers through the tight curls on his well-shaped head. With her heart hammering there was no other thought in her mind except to enjoy the blissful ecstasy of his kisses, his nearness. That was until her own desires flared into life.

She was aware of his arms tightening around her, of her own body crying out for fulfilment, and she began to struggle. But as his arms only tightened still more, she remained held tight against him, neither surrendering nor resisting until he felt her stiffen against the warmth and ardour of his longing.

She said, 'Please, Nick, I must go. It's getting late and I've enjoyed this evening. It's been wonderful.'

'But the time we've wasted! We have a lot to make up for, darling.' His hands were on her shoulders, holding her so hard that they hurt. 'You're going to marry me, so you'd better get used to the idea while I'm away. Because when I come back it won't be long before you're Mrs Nick Tabor, and I shan't take no for an answer.'

Davina framed his dark, stern face tenderly with her hands.

'Darling Nick! I want to marry you as much as you want to marry me, but don't you see it's because I love you so much that I couldn't bear the thought of something happening with Darren tearing my loyalties between you. You're so self-sufficient, and very much a man, whereas Darren isn't mature yet. He could go the wrong way so easily if he thought nobody cared.'

Nick kissed the palms of her hands. 'What am I to do with you?' he asked on a crooked smile. 'While your concern for your brother makes me love you all the more it also sends prickles running down my spine at the way you're going about it. He has to grow up, and quickly. Your mother spoiled him, now you're doing the same. I've never been one to compromise. In my book it's a sign of weakness and I don't intend to do it now.'

'But you expect me to. Oh, Nick!'

He smiled crookedly. 'I've never met a more obstinate woman in my life.'

'Not obstinate, only wanting desperately to do the right thing by my own family.'

His fingers curled around hers and he drew her arms around his neck.

'Don't look so unhappy about it,' he urged, seeing no answering twinkle in the wide eyes meeting his. 'All I want is your happiness, so I would hardly go against your wishes unless,' a grin, 'I had to.'

He spoke the last three words against her lips. Once again her very bones appeared to be melting at his touch. He knew that she longed desperately to give way to him, but she was physically and mentally tired, and the tug-of-war with her conscience was goading her almost to breaking point.

'I want to go home, please,' she said.

Nick set the car off swiftly through the night. The sky was gloriously tinted in rose and gold and stars were faintly twinkling in the summer sky.

He negotiated a difficult bend in the road, a road almost deserted because of the lateness of the hour.

'I've been a brute to keep you out so late,' he said. 'You'll be tired when you get up.'

'You must be tired too with jet lag from travelling home.'

'I'm tough. I can stand it better than you.' He sighed. 'It's hell not being free to take care of you. Suppose I don't see you again before I go away?'

Davina quivered. 'If ... if you want it that way,' she answered.

He braked at the flat and answered her tersely, 'I don't want it that way. It's up to you.'

He sat with his hands on the car wheel, not looking at her but staring straight ahead. Davina felt tired in mind and body and to have the added problem of yet another decision thrust upon her was the last straw.

She said recklessly, 'Let's call the whole thing off,' knowing as she said it that she did not mean it.

'Don't you dare say that again or even think it!' he threatened, turning to face her and hauling her against him. 'We belong together. This is what matters—and this—and this.

He kissed her roughly, drawing her resistance out of her and replacing it with something wonderful and full of meaning.

By now Davina was in no state to reason. She was

bemused and exhausted. She began to laugh helplessly with the tears starting in her eyes.

'For someone who's tired,' she gasped, 'you have
an enormous amount of energy! What are you like
when you're not tired?'

'I leave you to find that out for yourself when
we're married. Well, am I to see you again before
I go away?'

She looked at him with her lips tingling from his
kisses and found the thought of him going away
unbearable.

'I'd like to come to the airport to see you off.
Will that do?'

'A crust to a starving man,' he said wryly. 'I suppose it will have to suffice.'

The smile he gave her was nearly her undoing,
but the next moment he was out of the car and
helping her out. He opened the flat door for her
and stayed long enough to see her put a light on in
the lounge, then he was gone.

Cheryl took the news that Davina and Nick had
made up philosophically. She also agreed that Nick
was right to consult Darren and herself.

'Perhaps by then we shall know about the shop,
whether it's to be sold in the block or not,' she said
practically.

They were having breakfast the following morning.

'Would you mind so much if we had to give it
up?' Davina queried as she carefully buttered a
piece of toast.

Cheryl shrugged. 'I suppose I would, for your
sake. After all, you've put a lot into the business

and it's paying its way now.' She sipped the last of her fruit juice, then added thoughtfully, 'Have you ever thought that if it hadn't been for the flower shop you might never have met Nick?'

'No, I didn't, but I think we were fated to meet somewhere. In any case, if the shop is sold it won't be for a long time because the lease has about six months to run yet. We can do a lot in that time.'

Cheryl said darkly, 'Nick won't want you to work when you're married. You know that?'

'We'll cross that bridge when we come to it.' Davina laughed, not feeling as tired as she had expected to be after a very late night. In fact she felt quite elated.

'You know, I think I'm going to enjoy being married to Nick. Life with him will never be dull—I'm very sure about that.'

'It should be interesting to say the least. You're both very obstinate people,' Cheryl commented sardonically as she poured out coffee.

'Not obstinate. You make us sound like mules. Just firm. What about you? Have you any news about yourself and Rex?'

Cheryl sipped her coffee. 'I'll let you know when there's anything to report. From now on we have to concentrate on your forthcoming marriage. It'll be fun.'

Davina hoped Darren would take the same attitude. Thank goodness today was Friday and a busy day at the shop. She could put all her problems behind her and her feet up when she got home that evening.

She was flat out when Nick telephoned her that evening at ten o'clock.

'Not in bed, are you, darling?' he asked.

'No,' she answered above the deep beating of her heart. 'Are you?'

'No, I'm at the office getting ready to leave to-morrow morning at nine. I don't want you to come. You'll be whacked after a busy day today and then there's tomorrow.'

Did she detect a faint pleading in his voice? In Nick that was alarming.

'Try and stop me! I'll take a taxi to the airport.'

'Are you sure?'

The happiness in his voice touched a tender chord and she said lovingly, 'Of course I'm sure.'

'Then I'll pick you up in a taxi at eight. Will that be all right?'

'I'll be ready,' she promised.

And she was. Nick pulled her into the taxi beside him and into his arms as they fell into the back seat.

They kissed, then Davina pushed him away. 'The driver can see us through the mirror, and people will see us through the window,' she whispered with a high colour.

'Who cares?' he grinned. 'Let's hope some of your friends see us, then you'll have to marry me to save your good name.'

But he did not kiss her again. Instead he drew her against his broad chest and they sat together, close and loving. At the airport they found a corner table over looking the airfield and talked over coffee.

At least they tried to do, but did more looking at each other than making conversation.

'I suppose you want white and all the trimmings,' said Nick, adoring her with his eyes.

'Yes, I do. There's a kind of peace and tranquillity in a church wedding that you can't experience in a register office. My parents were married in church and were very happy. I want the same kind of happiness.'

He nodded in agreement. 'I know what you mean, a deep and fulfilling occasion that leaves a lasting impression of marriage being for ever.' He laughed as some thought occurred to him. 'I suppose you'll want to do the flowers yourself. I would prefer to give someone else the order to give you a rest.'

Davina lifted her chin. 'Of course I shall do them myself. But you're miles ahead of me. Don't you think you're rather rushing things?'

'Saving time,' he answered laconically.

Davina stood holding the chocolates, fruit and magazines Nick had bought her at the airport to watch him board the plane.

She watched the doors close, the wheels turn, the engines flash. Slowly the large plane moved from take-off position on the runway to test the engines, gradually its speed quickened, the fuselage flashed in the sun like a rocket and there was a perfect lightning take-off. Davina's heart had lifted with it as the plane disappeared into the sky.

She threw all she had into her work at the shop the following week. Nick telephoned her each night and she shuddered to think of the kind of telephone bill he ran up while doing so. He told her that his business abroad would take the best part of a week and that he would be back for the weekend.

Darren had agreed to come home for the weekend and Davina quivered with apprehension. Cheryl had been very quiet during the last week with

Davina sensing that their closeness was gradually widening into a rift too big for her to handle on her own. Time and again it had occurred to her that Cheryl might be in love with Nick and was trying to cover up by dating Rex.

Several times Davina had brought up the subject of her wedding, even suggesting lightly that they could make it a double one. Cheryl had refused to be drawn. There had been lighthearted moments when they had dressed the shop window with the model of a June bride as the centrepiece and Cheryl trailing around the shop in the veil.

It was heaven to see Nick again; heaven to discover that the old magic was still there when their eyes met, when their hands touched. Idiotically, she found herself looking to see if he had changed since he had been away. Here were the same steady grey eyes which hypnotised her senses, the masterful mouth, the fine lean cheeks sensitised by experience and not a few hard knocks. Davina had felt her heart take wing with love for him.

He had arrived late on Friday night to whisk her off to dine at an old inn in the country where they had a small private cubicle where they could hold hands across the table.

'Ten o'clock is rather late for a meal, isn't it?' Davina whispered as Nick seated her at the table.

Nick, teasing and vital, grinned at her across the snowy white cloth.

'They'll rustle something up for us,' he told her confidently.

And they did. The waitress was probably dead on her feet, but Nick's charm brought a glow to her tired face and she obliged. Fortunately they had

over-catered for a private party, so they were able
to provide an excellent meal.

Nick ordered champagne and told the waitress to
bring an extra glass for herself. The girl was overwhelmed and Davina smiled, knowing that the poor
dear would be more than overwhelmed by the size
of the tip Nick would give her later.

'To us,' said Nick, raising his glass, then showed
how ravenous he was by tucking in to a very enjoyable meal.

He was really concerned about Davina eating her
share, teasing her into trying everything that was
offered, from the poached salmon to the game pie
and cheeses which followed.

'I must take you in hand,' he told her with a
twinkle. 'You're too pale, too thin. You don't eat
enough. It's time you had someone to look after you.'

She said firmly, 'I am not pale nor thin and I
don't need feeding up.'

Their eyes met and held in a tingling shock to
Davina, who lowered her own against the mastery
in his. She quivered, seeing her life ahead not entering into the wide horizons she had expected but
narrowing down until they dwindled into a final
acceptance of Nick's mastery.

But it was not long before his charm got through
to her and she was chuckling over his audacious
stories of his travels.

'Has anyone told you what a delicious laugh you
have? I can't wait to show you off to my friends, and
my parents will adore you,' he told her.

She asked fearfully, 'Will they be coming to the
wedding?'

'Of course. Now about your ring. I'm going to buy

you another ring of your own choice this time. We must go out for the day shopping. Have you done any shopping for the wedding? I've already set the machine in progress. I shall need your birth certificate.'

'But I want my other ring back,' she insisted. 'I regard that as my true engagement ring.'

'It's at the flat. Have it by all means, but I'm still going to buy you another.'

'I can't come with you tomorrow. Saturday is too busy.'

'Monday, then, at ten sharp.'

Nervously, she asked, 'When will your parents be here?'

'In a day or so. You're going to love them. I pride myself on having the best in everything!'

Davina laughed. 'I like your ego—it's king-size! I suppose I ought to feel flattered to be the choice of a connoisseur for a wife.' She sobered. 'I want you to come to dinner tomorrow night at the flat. Darren and Cheryl will be there.'

'Ah yes, I must present my case,' he teased.

'You will be gentle with Darren, won't you? I mean ... don't antagonise him in any way.'

'I shall apologise quite nicely for taking his sister away.'

The next evening Davina and Cheryl managed to get away from the shop at five o'clock. After shopping they arrived at the flat to find Darren had already arrived with a fellow student for the weekend.

Darren was opening a tin of soup and Davina ushered his friend, Tony, into the lounge while she prepared a snack for them all.

'How could you do this to us, Darren?' she scolded as Cheryl got down to starting the dinner. 'I told you that Nick was coming to dinner. The number was even, just the four of us. Now we have an extra guest.'

Darren emptied the soup into a pan. 'We shan't be in the way,' he replied huffily. 'We'll go out.'

'That isn't the answer,' Davina wailed. 'We want to discuss the wedding.'

Darren mumbled, 'Well, he's not marrying me, so I don't see that it's important for me to be here.'

Davina placed tomatoes on a plate on the kitchen table.

'If I marry Nick,' she said quietly, 'it will concern us all as a family. Don't you like Nick?'

'I don't really know him, do I?'

Darren continued to stir the soup in the pan while Davina started to cut bread and butter.

She said, 'Dinner is at eight. This is just something to tide us over.'

She set out knives and forks with a feeling that the evening would be a disaster as far as Darren was concerned. He had gone out with his friend Tony when everything was set for Nick to arrive.

'Really, it's too bad of Darren to act like this,' grumbled Cheryl. 'I shall feel as if I'm playing gooseberry with you and Nick. Rex is away so I can't ask him to make a foursome. Shall I go out?'

'Whatever for?' Both girls had dressed for the evening. 'Come on, let's go into the lounge and have a drink to cheer us up while we wait for Nick.'

The room was welcoming and cosy with flower arrangements in bowls and vases giving the place a lived-in air. Davina looked around as she poured out tomato juice for Cheryl and herself with the sharpened perception of waiting for a guest. The room with its comfortable suite and bright cushions was not in the class of Nick's flat and she could imagine that his parents' home was much grander.

Cheryl said as she accepted her drink, 'You look thoughtful. Not changing your mind about Nick, are you?'

Davina sat down gracefully beside her and sipped her drink.

'No,' she answered firmly.

As she spoke Davina felt her pride come back to strengthen her. She was going to marry Nick. She was not going to allow Darren or anyone else rule her life for her. She had battled her way to where she now was, she would fight for her marriage with the same resolve.

When Nick arrived Cheryl discreetly vanished to the kitchen. Davina thrilled to the firm pressure of his lips on her own and found herself loving him more than ever.

He did not ask where Darren was, and once or twice during the meal she gave him openings to ask about him, but he did not mention Darren at all and it was clear he was not going to.

Deliberately, with that inflexibility which was characteristic of him, Nick made the evening a happy one. He was an excellent raconteur of amusing incidents and he kept both girls entertained. After Cheryl had gone to bed he sat with Davina to discuss their future.

First of all they were going out into the country the next day. Nick was taking a picnic prepared by Mrs Flowers. On Monday they were going shopping. He had arranged for their wedding and wanted to take Davina's birth certificate with him.

Clasped in his arms, while she was so near him, while she was so conscious of her love for him, Davina could not think clearly. She was allowing him to take the initiative again and it worried her. Since her parents had died she had proved herself to be capable of handling family matters without being oppressively efficient in the many exigencies they presented.

If Nick was prepared to take her life over without even a by your leave, he would certainly want to take over Darren's. That would not suit Darren. What could she do but hope for the best?

Nick was masterful, but that was part of him being Nick, part of the way he was kissing her hungrily, sealing her lips with his own.

'Don't talk,' he said. 'Just go along with me, and don't look so preoccupied as you've done all evening. You want to marry me, I know you do.'

'Of course I do,' she reassured him frantically. 'I love you so much.'

He kissed her again, fiercely until his lips bruised and she held back her head eventually to give a small laugh; low, utterly sweet, utterly loving.

'Oh, Nick!' she whispered. 'You're the kind of lover I would feel safer married to.'

Darkly, he said, 'You have been warned.'

Darren had not returned when Nick took his leave, so Davina waited up for him. Both boys came back in the small hours, only slightly tipsy. They had been to a dance and had enjoyed themselves immensely.

After telling them to be careful not to waken

Cheryl, Davina gave them coffee and biscuits and then told Darren she wanted to talk to him.

Tony went to bed while Darren sprawled across a chair in the kitchen.

'Enjoy your evening?' he asked insolently.

Davina put the used dishes in the sink and poured hot water on them from the tap.

'Yes, I did,' she replied. 'You evidently enjoyed yours, so why shouldn't I? You're being dreadfully childish.'

'Because I wouldn't stay in to meet your intended?'

'Because you refuse to face facts. You can't run away from life, Darren. You have to face it sooner or later. You're jealous of Nick, aren't you? I don't know why.'

'He's breaking up the happy home, isn't he?'

'No, he isn't,' Davina replied indignantly. 'He's adding to it. Nothing will be changed. I shall keep the shop on, Cheryl will be here in the flat when you come home. I shall be at home while Nick is away until we have a house.'

'And how long will it be before you have children?'

Davina's face went scarlet. 'There won't be any children for a while.'

Darren said, 'I wish I could believe that.'

CHAPTER NINE

IT was hardly the weather for a picnic, but Nick was optimistic about the strong cool winds and the rather doubtful skies when they set off in his car. But being with Nick was fun under any circumstances and Davina could only giggle when he said something unprintable as an unexpected gust of wind swept away the tablecloth before they could pin it down.

The canvas protection awning, though securely pinned down, was the next to be blown away, with one flap soaring high above Davina's head as she reached out for it. She laughed until her sides ached while Nick struggled on manfully.

From time to time Nick said one or two more unprintable things, especially when the tablecloth was carried away bearing with it all the things laid out for their meal. Then came a heavy downpour of rain quite unexpectedly and they made for the car, drenched to the skin after collecting all the picnic equipment.

In the car there was laughter and kisses. Davina's face glowed. For the first time with Nick there had been no hidden shadows in her eyes, no hint of doubt, no drawing away from him. She had been just young, exuberant, natural, and joyful.

To Nick she had never been more desirable than now, with laughter in her eyes and her hair, wet and tangled, curling around her flushed eager face.

When he reached out for her she laughed with the gleam of white small even teeth and he caught her to his heart. Almost sombrely he was kissing her wet face, loving the sweetness beneath the dampness; crushing her to him, her soft throat, bright eyes and curved body and fiercely loving.

Davina came to earth first. 'Let's see, what were we eating when the deluge came. I know, apple pie. Do you want some?'

'Sounds awfully banal after the caviar of love,' he remarked wryly.

Davina blushed delightfully. 'But we've only experienced the preliminaries of love yet.'

Nick grinned and reached for a piece of the apple pie.

'We could have the real thing,' he said audaciously, his eyes twinkling. 'I might tell you you've been very near to it happening each time I take you in my arms.'

'Nick Tabor,' she said primly, 'you are impossible!'

He kissed the end of her nose. 'And you, my sweet, are adorable. I can't wait to make you mine.'

On Monday they went shopping to buy the ring, plus an engagement ring of her choice. She lingered reluctantly over a tray of the latter.

'I don't want a second engagement ring. I already have this one,' she whispered, holding up her left hand to show the ring he had returned to her finger.

'What about this one?' Nick selected a beautiful diamond ring from the tray as if he had not heard. 'Try it for size.'

He took hold of her hand and pushed the ring

gently on above the other, determined to have his own way. It was one of the most expensive on the tray and Davina gasped.

The sales assistant beamed his approval. 'A truly beautiful ring, madam. The stone is flawless. You would find it an excellent investment.'

She said stubbornly, 'If I have to have a ring then it must be of my own choice. I'll have an eternity ring, please.'

Nick grinned, 'The choice is yours, my sweet.'

And so it was for the rest of the day. Nick escorted her to the fashion salons to buy her trousseau and nodded his approval at her choice. In between he chose expensive items which Davina had passed over, to be included.

He had excellent taste and Davina wondered how often he had been with his girl-friends on a shopping spree. It was naïve, she knew, to think that he had not had any affairs. His good looks, his charm, his ability to look well in his clothes in a way that everything he wore was correct forged a weapon against which even the coldest of women would wilt.

The shop assistants they encountered were clearly captivated by his cool, nonchalant charm, and Davina felt many an envious glance in her direction when that beautiful deep voice expressed an opinion about a particular garment.

It was over lunch that he sprang his surprise.

'We're going out into the country to meet my parents. They arrived home during the weekend and we're going down now to see them.'

Davina stared at him in dismay. 'But why didn't you tell me so that I could put something special on? I mean, you ... you just don't spend a morning shopping, then ... then stagger off to meet your future in-laws!'

Nick flicked a glance drenched with pleasure at the slender figure in pale green with white accessories. The sun was on the silky brown hair and the green eyes with their adorable tilt were filled with alarm.

His long slender fingers curled around his wine glass as he said lazily, 'I didn't tell you before because I knew you'd spend a sleepless night wondering about it and what to wear—as if it mattered. You look enchanting as always and my parents are going to love you.'

'Nick Tabor,' she muttered through clenched teeth, 'I could kill you! It didn't occur to you, did it, that I might have wanted to take your mother some flowers or something?'

'Good lord,' he said with some amusement. 'Mother doesn't expect flowers, she's surrounded by them.'

'You mean a market garden or something?' she queried, brightening.

This was too much for Nick. He laughed as if at some good joke.

'Why don't you wait and see?' he suggested.

Davina watched the countryside, green and inviting, from the car window and hoped that his parents would welcome her as beautifully. She thought of her own mother and her love for her only son. Would Nick's mother resent her taking him from the family nest as she was sure her mother would have done?

Nick's deep voice broke into her thoughts. 'Not

worrying about my parents, are you?'

'Naturally I'm perturbed about it. What engaged girl wouldn't be? While I appreciate your thoughtfulness in not telling me until the last moment I still have that funny feeling in the pit of my stomach.'

'But, darling, you're not marrying them, you're marrying me.'

'Of course I am. That's why I'm worried.'

They were passing a neat little village and Nick suddenly slowed down to pull in at a public telephone booth.

'Come with me,' he said as he braked.

He dwarfed the inside of the telephone booth by his width and height and he took the opportunity to hold her against him as he dialled a number. Then he rested the telephone on his shoulder while he felt in his pocket for the money to put in the slot.

'Hello, Mother. I shall be seeing you in a very short time. We're on the way. Here's Davina to speak to you.'

He thrust the receiver into Davina's hand and closed his own over it.

'My mother, darling,' he said.

Davina swallowed nervously on a dry throat. 'Hello, Mrs Tabor. Nick has just broken the news that we're on the way to see you. I hope it isn't inconvenient.'

She covered the mouthpiece with her hand and hissed, 'I don't know what to say, you idiot!' then she listened.

'Nick told us he would be bringing you today. I wanted him to bring you to lunch, but he explained about the shopping. I trust everything went well. I suppose Nick took charge.'

There was laughter and warmth in Mrs Tabor's voice and Davina relaxed visibly.

'He took charge all right, but everything is fine. See you soon.'

'Well?' Nick asked as he took the receiver from her to replace it. 'That wasn't too bad, was it? Now you aren't strangers any longer. Quite nice, isn't she, my mother?'

'She sounds sweet, but you might have told me what you had in mind instead of hauling me into the telephone booth. I'm beginning to wonder what I've let myself in for.'

'I'll tell you,' he whispered against her mouth. 'The most wonderful time you've ever had.'

Ardent moments passed until they were brought to earth by an irate elderly woman tapping on the window of the telephone booth. Davina's face was scarlet as they left the booth, but Nick was quite unruffled.

He apologised politely and held open the door to let the woman in. Needless to say she was bowled over by his charm. Davina thought helplessly, no woman can resist him, so how can I be expected to?

She saw what Nick had meant by the flowers, for the double gates already opened for their arrival led to a beautiful garden of velvet lawns and a glorious display of flowers.

As Nick braked at the front door a woman came to greet them to stand beneath the entrance of fluted stone. The house was Georgian, mellow, dignified and not too big.

Like her son, Nina Tabor was a woman of infinite charm and intelligence. She sparkled with the same vitality that held a healthy outlook on life, having known perfect health herself. Davina liked her on sight, liked her natural way. She was tall, elegant but not ostentatious. Her fair hair had a sprinkling of grey in the soft waves which fell naturally around a clear-skinned face remarkably unlined. Davina felt instinctively that here was a woman she could trust, one who would make a good friend.

Nick kissed her cheek and she turned to take Davina's hand as he introduced her.

'Welcome into the family, Davina,' she said with a hint of laughter in her voice. 'I've been longing to meet you, for Nick has told us so much about you in his letters.'

Davina said shyly, 'I hope you're better for your stay abroad.'

'Much better, thanks. It's good to be home, though. I don't know where my husband is. Look, Nick, perhaps Davina would like to freshen up. Take her upstairs while I find your father.'

They walked upstairs, and Davina turned to face Nick as he stopped at a bathroom door.

'Lovely house,' she said. 'Very homely.'

He drew her into his arms. 'Isn't it?' he answered slowly in between kissing the side of her neck. 'We'll have one like it if you like.'

She said seriously, 'But we are staying at your flat for a while after we're married, aren't we?'

'It will be a bit cramped. You'll be glad to get out of it.'

'I won't ... at least, not for a while.'

He lifted his head and gazed at her in surprise.

'Aren't you eager for a place of your own?'

'Of course I am. But your flat is conveniently near to the flower shop.'

'So what?' he asked curtly. 'You won't be going to the flower shop when we're married.'

'For a little while. I must help Cheryl to get into the scheme of things before I give it up. After all, you're insisting on an early wedding. You have to make some concession.'

'I shall have my way on this,' he said. 'No wife of mine is going to work. I have a certain amount of entertainment to do in my job and I want you there.'

'I will be,' she promised, winding her arms around his neck. 'Just try to get rid of me, Mr Tabor, and you'll see.'

Nick answered by kissing her very thoroughly, then he opened the bathroom door and gave her a gentle push inside.

'See you downstairs,' he said.

Davina washed and dried herself on one of the white fluffy towels and after making herself presentable went downstairs. Nick was at the foot of the stairs waiting for her and he escorted her into the lounge to meet his father.

Waiting for them, John Tabor smiled at the slender Davina with the sun slanting across the room on her shiny hair highlighting the green eyes, staring at him apprehensively.

'This is a very pleasant occasion,' he said, holding out his hand to her. 'I've been waiting for this day for a long time and it's certainly been worth waiting for. Delighted to meet you, my dear.'

Davina gave him her hand, hesitated for a moment, then she was giving him an affectionate smile and her eyes with their enchanting slight tilt laughed up at him.

'I'm pleased to meet you too,' she said. 'Did you enjoy your stay abroad?'

He assured her that he had but was glad to be back. His grey eyes, so like Nick's, gently mocked her.

He said, 'Had we have known there was going to be a welcome surprise like this at the end of it we might have come sooner. We've been wanting Nick to settle down for a long time.'

Davina, conscious of Nick's tall figure beside her, said,

'You don't think it's too soon?'

'It's beautifully soon,' Nick said softly above her ear as he put a possessive arm around her. 'Don't you think so, Dad?'

His father laughed. 'My advice is grab her before someone else does!'

Nina Tabor was watching them in amusement. 'Stop talking about Davina as though she isn't here. Let's go out and sit in the garden. Pity to waste the time indoors.'

On the front lawn of the house Davina and Nina sat in garden chairs while the two men lay on the grass. While the two women talked about things which interested them the two men discussed business.

They had tea and later dinner which they went indoors for. There were just the four of them in the dining room with its tall French windows looking out on to the gardens. The table with tall candles in heavy silver candlesticks sparkled with crystal and beautiful tableware on gay mats.

The meal, the wine, was excellent. There were no awkward moments of people meeting for the first time.

'After dinner we'll go for a walk,' Nick had said.

They strolled through the grounds arm in arm in the cool evening air.

Davina said, 'I like your parents. They're sweet.'

'They'll soon be yours,' he answered. 'Three weeks from now. I thought we could spend our wedding night here and go away the following day. As we shall have the wedding celebrations here I thought it would be more convenient.'

They had sat down on a garden seat. It was not quite dark with the moon casting a waxen glow over the silent garden and giving the flowers an artificial bloom.

Davina, meeting his mocking eyes and reading knowledge of her embarrassment in them, felt the colour rush warmly to her face.

'You appear to have arranged everything. Aren't I to be consulted?'

He laughed and hugged her against him. 'We're getting married, so I don't see that it matters who makes the arrangements—especially as you're fighting shy of it.'

She lifted her chin. 'That isn't fair! I happen to have commitments. I just can't drop anything at the drop of a hat. There's the shop.'

'Ah yes, the shop. The bone of contention between us. It will have to go unless Cheryl wants to keep it on which I very much doubt.'

Davina felt her heart lurch and she stared down at the ground with troubled eyes. Family was invading the sweetness and passion they shared, she and Nick. The evening breeze stirred her hair and a cold hand seemed to touch her heart.

'I'll have you know,' she managed in a choked little voice, 'I've built the business up. It's been my baby. Now you write it off just like that!'

'That's right. You'll have real babies in exchange.'

Davina twisted herself from his hold and stood up to walk a few paces from him.

Presenting him with her back, she said in a low voice,

'I can't be as casual as you about it. I can't tear up my roots in three weeks flat, neither can I expect Cheryl and Darren to do the same. You're being so matter-of-fact about it.'

'Of course I'm being matter-of-fact about it. It's the way I am. One has to do things deliberately in order to get things done. I've never been one who believes in compromise. You need someone to take care of you, and I'm doing just that.'

He had moved behind her to put his hands on her shoulders and Davina held her breath at the deceptive lightness of his grip. Part of her wanted to say that the wedding was off, to say nasty things to drive him away, while the other part was goading her to lie back against him—to end the deadlock.

Clenching her hands, Davina knew that she had no valid argument. Either she loved Nick or she didn't. And she did love him better than life itself. A whisper of common sense urged her to take what the gods offered, but there was no peace for her if she did. There would always be Darren to condemn her.

'Davina.' His voice was low and musical, turning

the sound of her name on his lips into a thing of beauty. 'There's nothing to worry about. Everything will work out.'

Slowly he turned her round to face him. 'All these foolish notions you have about your family—they'll be taken care of.'

'You don't understand.' She lifted large troubled eyes, green pools in the lovely paleness of her face. 'I have to do this thing my way or not at all.'

He smiled down at her. 'But you won't, my darling. You'll put yourself into my hands—and do you know why? Because you love me.' As he captured her startled upward glance there was a steely purpose in his eyes, to be banished almost at once by a return to his old derision. 'Darling, this is your life and mine. We belong together.'

His arms closed around her, gathering her into a world of protection that only contained them both. And as his lips claimed hers Davina knew that with him lay life's fulfilment and all that there was of everything that mattered in life.

The weeks that followed went in a dream for Davina. At times she was in a panic to see how quickly time was flying. At other times she told herself that when they were married she would manage Nick. If he loved her he would at least grant her some things she wanted, like keeping on the shop and going there while he was away. By continuing to work up the business she could sell the good will when the time came and the proceeds would add to the investments they already had in the family. Even Darren would hardly object to that. There would be money enough for him to complete his studies and also a nest egg for his future, and it would not be Nick's money. It would be his by right of family.

They were to be married on the Saturday. The shop was open until Friday night for Davina and Cheryl to attend to all the orders. It was an exhausting time, what with the rehearsals for the wedding in the village church attended by Nick and his parents through the years, and everything else the wedding entailed.

By the time her wedding day arrived Davina was a bundle of nerves bordering on hysteria. Not that there was anything to worry about. The dress was a dream and Nick telephoned in the morning to ask how she was feeling.

Juleen arrived to help with her husband, who took Darren off to see his new car. Darren was to give away the bride, who was thinking for the umpteenth time that noon was far too late for the ceremony. It was too wearing on the nerves, Davina told herself. Far better to get it over early in the morning and go away.

Then suddenly there she was in a breathtaking wedding dress of white lace and a flowing veil fitting snugly over the thick brown cap of silky, shining hair. Her trembling fingers closed around the bouquet and she was ready.

The small country church was beautiful as it basked in the sun. Rainbow beams of sunlight spraying through the windows warmed her slender frame as she laid pearl-tipped fingers on Darren's arm to walk gracefully down the aisle. Cheryl, in cherry red velvet, was close behind her as the organ pealed.

Staring down at the blood red roses and fern making a splash against the white of her gown, Davina was aware of a small select congregation comprising mostly Nick's family and friends. And he was there waiting for her with the sun resting on the wide shoulders and the tight cap of curls.

His suit was an impeccable grey and he looked aggressively handsome and very male. He turned his head as she reached his side and Davina saw the subtle perceptiveness of his steady grey gaze change to one of worshipping adoration. Their eyes met, clung, and from then on everything passed with a dreamlike quality for Davina.

When he slipped the ring on her finger she felt the peace and love of the church was over her. Then his lips met hers in a kiss that was skilfully casual, a kiss that could in no way be compared with those later in the car going to the reception. His embrace then was enchanting, his face smoothly shaved and fragrant with after-shave lotion was cool. His kisses lingered until she was out of breath.

'Well, Mrs Tabor,' he whispered with a hint of mockery, 'the first real kisses from your husband. Love me?'

Davina, beyond words, put her hand in his and curled her fingers round it until they reached the house.

There in the entrance hall banked high with flowers they welcomed their guests as they arrived. Lunch was laid out in the dining room with Nick's parents joining the guests as they all trooped in.

Nick's hand was firm over hers as they cut the cake and there were the usual speeches. Nick was all sparkle and kinetic magnetism while Davina quietly glowed.

But by the time the long lunch was over Davina was relying on forced energy. The excitement and exhausting preparations along with work at the shop had drained her. It was Nick who had drawn her aside and told her to go to their room to rest for an hour or so in the afternoon.

The suggestion had been more than welcome, for Davina did not know what was heavier, the ring on her finger or her painfully throbbing head. Their room had two spacious bow windows that gave panoramic views of the countryside. Davina found herself looking out on scenes familiar to Nick as a boy which she took in as vaguely as the big bed situated between the two bay windows. It spelt rest and peace for a while.

She was awakened by the running of water through wedding dress, but the cool sheets were heaven to her tired limbs. Gradually she relaxed and closed her eyes.

She was awakened by the runing of water through the pipes in the house, which meant that the guests were freshening up for the buffet and dance arranged for the evening. It was seven o'clock by her watch and Davina looked at it clear-eyed.

Her headache had gone and she felt utterly rested. She took her time under the shower, dressed leisurely in her fine lace and silk undies and shook out one of her new evening dresses, part of her trousseau. She was getting into it when Nick strode into the room.

'Let me zip you up,' he said as she stepped into the dress and hastened to pull it up.

Before he did so he bent to kiss the smooth skin of her back.

'How are you feeling? I came in about an hour ago to change and you were sleeping like a baby.'

She looked at his reflection behind her own in the dressing table mirror. His face had the healthy bronze laid on by countless sojourns abroad and his curly head looked almost white in contrast. His eyes met hers in a slow smile and his hands came round to cup her firm small bust.

'Pity we have to go down again,' he whispered with his lips against the side of her neck.

She said lightly, 'This is my day, so it has to last as long as possible.'

Reluctantly he dropped his hands. 'Which reminds me,' he said, and drew a flat packet from his pocket. 'A present for my bride.'

He placed the necklace around her throat and fastened it expertly.

'What about a kiss?' he said.

'Oh, Nick!' she cried. 'You've already bought me a ring. You're spoiling me!'

Her arms slid around his neck and it was some minutes before they came to earth again.

'Roll on tonight,' Nick groaned as he reluctantly let her go.

The evening passed without incident with everybody enjoying themselves. Music was provided by a record player and the buffet next to the room cleared for dancing was well attended.

Davina wandered among the guests with Nick as champagne flowed freely. Darren, she noticed, was drinking his share. He was with Cheryl and a group of young people and Davina realised that she did not know half the guests while Nick appeared to know them all.

Darren and Cheryl left around midnight with Juleen and Jocelyn who were giving them a lift home. Darren was unusually merry and Davina caught his arm as he staggered to the car.

'You'll have a bad head tomorrow,' she told him.

He shook her arm off roughly. 'I bet you will too,' he growled rudely. 'Don't forget—no babies.'

Davina was still trembling when the car had gone. Then Nick's arm was around her.

'Cold?' he asked gently.

She laughed and shivered. 'Not really. Just someone walking over my grave.'

He lifted a brow. 'That's a strange expression to use on our wedding night. Come on, let's find Mother and Dad—it's long past your bedtime.'

CHAPTER TEN

DAVINA opened her eyes to a room flooded with sunlight. The place beside her in the big bed was empty with only the indentation in the pillow to show that Nick had been there. Nick! her heart cried out desolately.

It was some minutes before she could force herself to go through the events of the previous evening. Then step by step she went through it remorselessly. Most of the guests had gone when they met up with Nina and Jocelyn to say goodnight and to thank them for all they had done.

Nina had taken Davina aside for a moment.

She said warmly, 'I've haven't seen Nick look so happy for a long time. Thank you, my dear, for making him so.'

Tears forced their way beneath Davina's eyelids as she closed her eyes. She liked Nick's parents so much. Nick had got caught up with the last of the guests who were taking their leave when she went to bed.

In the quietness of the big pleasant room Davina prepared for bed, slipping on the pretty nightdress with its peasant-style stringed neck. She had slipped in between the cool sheets when Nick came up. She lay silent as he went into the bathroom and by the time he got into bed beside her, Davina was palpitating.

'Darling,' he had whispered, gathering her gently into his arms.

His kisses had been exploratory at first as leisurely he had untied the drawn neck of her nightdress in order to slip it down her recumbent form. It was then that Davina had stiffened in his arms. Feverishly it had seemed to her that she could hear Darren's voice: No babies.

Nick had sensed her withdrawal instantly, but he was tolerant to a degree. In vain, he had tried to awaken a response in her. He had been in turn gentle and rough.

She was appalled at her own behaviour. Miserably she put an arm out to the side of the bed where her negligé lay on the back of a pretty velvet upholstered tub chair. Then swinging her legs out of bed she hastily shrugged into it. Her nightdress lay in a forlorn heap at the foot of the bed where Nick had thrown it, a symbol of her broken dreams.

A tap on the door sent her scurrying into bed as the door opened to admit Nick with a tray. He was fully dressed and looked his usual immaculate self.

'Oh, Nick!' she cried, pushing herself up in bed. 'I feel awful. I . . . I can't explain . . . I mean, I . . .'

'Forget it,' he said, placing the tray on the bed. 'I've brought you your breakfast.'

Her green eyes were swimming with tears as he sat down on the edge of the bed to face her and lift a gentle hand to her tumbled hair.

'You look more a child than ever with tears in your eyes,' he teased, ruffling the heavy waves of hair and dabbing the tears hovering on the thick, long lashes with his handkerchief. 'There's nothing to cry about—after all, nerves are quite common in emotional situations. You've been doing far too much at the shop and I might have rushed you into a marriage you weren't ready for. How old are you, twenty-four?' The smile did not reach his eyes. 'Probably a late developer.'

Davina gave a beautiful misty smile and Nick settled himself against her charms. Fondling his clean-shaven chin thoughtfully, he said, 'I think I'll retract that last remark, because I don't think you are.'

He reached for the coffee pot and proceeded to fill the cups on the tray with steaming liquid. The aroma of freshly ground coffee beans filled the room, bringing with it a homely atmosphere which made Davina feel more normal.

'You don't think I'm what?' she queried, accepting the cup he offered.

'That you're a late developer. Not when I recall how you've always returned my kisses,' he answered, adding sugar to his cup. 'In fact I would say you could be a real sizzler. So why the frozen mitt?'

Davina gazed at the tight curls on his head as he drank his coffee. How often she had dreamed of drowning in his arms on their first night and thrusting her fingers through those curls.

She sipped part of her coffee. There was nothing else for it, she owed him complete honesty. He had been honest with her. She had to tell him, explain about Darren.

Her hands were trembling so much she had to put down her cup.

'I was afraid,' she burst out.

'Afraid?' Nick echoed as if he did not know the meaning of the word. 'Of me?'

'No, no.' Davina shook her head emphatically. 'Of the outcome. I didn't want any babies ... at least, not yet.'

Nick put down his empty cup to stare at her incredulously.

'And you thought I'd give you one on our first night? You are naïve, aren't you?'

She shook her head angrily. 'No, I'm not. Don't treat me like a child!'

'Then don't behave like one.'

'I'm not. Don't you see? I'm just as healthy and capable of feeling deeply as you are. Also I'm head over heels in love with my husband.'

He rose suddenly from the bed to stroll across the room to the window.

'I wish I could believe that,' he said, presenting his broad shoulders and the back of his well shaped head.

'It's true.'

'Then why did you marry me if you didn't want children?'

'But I do want children, only ...'

He turned round slowly from the window to face her with his expression in the shade.

'Only what?' he insisted.

'If you must know, it's something to do with the shop and Darren. Naturally I've tried to do the best for Cheryl and Darren moneywise. I ... I wanted to go on a little longer in order to give them security if only in a small way. If you hadn't come along I would have worked the shop up into something worth while.'

He said harshly, 'You mean that Darren is demanding money from you. Has he got himself into debt? If he's been blackmailing you I'll tan the hide off him!'

'It's nothing like that. He would have been too proud to let you help him.'

'So, in a way, he really did blackmail you into keeping on the shop? I've never heard anything so sickening in my life! That settles it.'

He strode to the door and Davina called out, 'Where are you going?'

He turned and his eyes were grey granite. 'To put your affairs in order. That talk with your family is long overdue.'

He was half out of the door when she said quietly, 'If you do what I think you're going to do I'll never forgive you.'

'We aren't exactly on matey terms as it is, are we?' said Nick.

Davina sat for a long time staring at the closed door. Thoughts were chasing each other in her head like demented hornets. Where would Nick go first, to see Cheryl or Darren? Darren would be at the flat for the weekend. After last evening he could possibly be in bed nursing a hangover, which meant he would not be easy to manage.

Davina got out of bed quickly after putting the tray with the untouched breakfast at the bottom of the bed. She had to get to the flat as soon as possible. There was no knowing what would happen with Nick in his present mood and Darren.

The thought of transport from a house in the country did occur to her as she washed and dressed. Also an excuse was needed for her to explain her reason for going home.

Nina was crossing the hall as she went downstairs.

Her smile was fond. 'Good morning, Davina. Nick said you were having a lie in this morning.'

'I never could lie in bed in the mornings—besides, I have to go to the flat for something I want.' She hesitated, relieved to see that her mother-in-law was not in the least curious about it. Then she continued, 'I suppose there are taxis, are there?'

Nina nodded. 'What a pity you didn't mention it to Nick—he's just left. However, Jocelyn has to go to the hospital this morning and John is driving up to go with him to see a new orthopaedic wing which has just been installed there. You can travel with your father-in-law. Isn't that nice?'

Davina hugged her. 'It's so nice having you for my relations. I'm sure Cheryl and Darren will feel the same. I'm ready to go when Father is.'

John Tabor drove the big car with the same ease of manner used by his son.

As they sped along the countryside, he said, 'We were beginning to think Nick would never marry. See, what is he, six years older than you, which makes him thirty. While he's had affairs he never seemed inclined to settle down. He has this bachelor flat in London and he spent most weekends when he was at home with us.'

He chuckled so much like Nick that Davina wanted to hug him.

'He liked to keep us guessing about whether his affairs would end in marriage. We had an idea that one day he would just present us with a bride he'd married in some registrar's office. He was always a happy child, full of devilment but always taking his punishment like a man. He was never cruel. On the other hand he would never compromise.'

Listening to him, Davina had the feeling of having failed Nick and Darren, but this was no time to wallow in self-reproach; she had to prevent a confrontation between her husband and her brother.

She turned to gaze over familiar scenes and realised that they were not far from the flat. Her tone was quiet and introspective.

'I'm lucky to have a husband and in-laws whom I like as well as love.'

'You're a romantic,' he teased.

'Most women are,' she returned lightly. 'Some men are, too. I think you are.'

'You're right, I am,' he replied ironically. 'I'm still very much in love with my wife.'

Davina wanted to say that she was very much in love with Nick, but they had nearly reached the flat and her companion had to pull up short to allow an ambulance to pass at speed.

Suddenly Davina shivered at some unknown fear and the next moment she was clutching her father-in-law's arm as they neared the flat above the flower shop.

Her voice sounded hoarse with shock. 'That fire engine ahead,' she croaked. 'It appears to be outside the shop.'

'I'm afraid it is,' John Tabor replied in level tones. 'Don't worry, they seem to be concentrating on the rooms above the shop.'

'That's our flat!' she cried. 'Do hurry, please!'

He pulled up as near as he was allowed to and Davina was out of the car. A thick grey plume of smoke was coming from the flat and the firemen were playing their hoses on it.

'You can't go up there, miss.'

One of the firemen spreading out the hose on the ground straightened to catch hold of her arm as she made for the side entrance by the shop window.

'But my sister and brother are up there. I must go up to them!' she cried, trying to free herself.

'Not any more they're not,' the man replied. 'They've gone to the hospital.'

'Both of them?' she gasped.

'There were three of them, including the young chap who carried them out.'

Davina was hardly conscious of her father-in-law coming to join her. She swallowed on a deadly fear.

'Are they badly ... hurt?' she asked.

'Suffering from fumes, I'd say. Lucky the young chap who gave the alarm came along when he did. He did a very brave thing. He'd already got them out when we arrived.'

Davina could have fallen against her father-in-law, but somehow she managed to stand on quivering legs.

'And ... and they all three have gone to hospital?' she said.

The fireman nodded. 'Overcome with fumes they were.'

Davina looked at Nick's father. His face was an angular mask.

'I ... I'm sorry,' she told him. 'Will you take me to the hospital?'

With unwonted gentleness he placed an arm around her shoulders and led her back to his car.

He said as he started the car, 'I don't think much damage has been done to your flat. The roof was intact and the men appeared to have the fire under control.'

Tonelessly, she said, 'It doesn't matter, does it, not against the lives of three people?'

'No, it doesn't, my child,' he agreed. 'Let us pray that we find them unharmed.'

His studied calmness did not deceive Davina, who knew that he was worried sick about Nick. As for herself and her own feelings, she did not dare to think about any of them.

The girl on reception at the hospital directed them to a corridor where a Sister came to meet them on whispering feet.

Her smile at Davina was kind. 'Mrs Tabor, you can go in to see your sister—she's in a side ward here. Mr Tabor, you're to come with me.'

Davina was shown into a ward and she caught the Sister's arm in anguish.

'My brother and my husband,' she cried in distress. 'Are they . . .?'

Sister said kindly, 'Please go in to see your sister. I'll come for you in a few moments.'

With a last agonising look at her father-in-law who nodded his head reassuringly, Davina went into the small ward.

Cheryl lay looking very pale but none the worse for her unpleasant experience.

She gave a wan smile. 'Sorry to spoil your honey-moon, Davina,' she said huskily. 'I got off lightly, thanks to Nick.'

'But how did it happen? Juleen and Jocelyn took you home, didn't they?'

Davina sank down on the chair beside the bed and looked helplessly at her sister.

Cheryl said, 'Yes, they did. Darren wasn't really drunk. He was acting grown up as usual. He walked into the flat and sat in the lounge while I made coffee. I left him drinking it and went to bed. He must have lighted a cigarette and then fallen asleep. His arm was along the arm of the chair and the cigarette smouldered, hence the fumes.'

'And Darren and Nick?' Davina held her breath as her green eyes searched Cheryl's face in anguish. 'How are they?'

Cheryl shook her head. 'I don't know. They won't tell me.' Suddenly her face crumpled and she began to cry quietly. 'I blame myself for leaving Darren in the lounge instead of insisting on him going to bed.'

'You're not to say that,' Davina said, choking back her own tears and giving Cheryl her handkerchief. 'Here, blow your nose and tell me what Nick did.'

Cheryl blew her nose and dried her eyes. 'I don't know. I woke up in hospital after he'd carried me out of the flat. I remember dazedly seeing his smoke-blackened face when I was lifted into the ambulance, that's all.'

Davina bit hard on her trembling lip. Her voice shook.

'Darren would get the worst of it, because ... because he was sitting in the smouldering chair.'

She was fighting back the tears when the door opened and Sister said quietly, 'Will you come with me, Mrs Tabor?'

Gallantly, Davina squeezed Cheryl's hand, then rose on her trembling legs to force them forward. The next moment she was stepping from the ward into someone's arms. They closed warmly around

her and all she could do was to cling and go on
clinging.

'Oh, Nick!' she cried through her tears. 'It's
heaven to see you again. Are you all right? Let me
look at you.'

His arms slackened as she lifted her head with a
look of horror at his grimy face and hair. His teeth
were very white as he grinned reassuringly.

'I'm fine,' he said. 'You aren't getting rid of me
that easily.'

Tears of thankfulness welled in her eyes and a
spasm of pain contracted her face.

'And Darren?' she asked in a scared whisper.

'Darren is going to be fine. He has a strong con-
stitution that's going to carry him through.'

Her legs went weak under her and Nick was
holding her close. He felt the fragrance of her hair
against his face, the salt of her happy tears on his
lips as he held her slim suppleness against him.

At last the world had righted around her. There
was a lot to be explained, but for the moment
Davina was ecstatically happy in the knowledge
that her loved ones were safe and recovering. Nothing else was more important than that.

At last she said, 'I want to see Darren.'

'So you shall, but right now we're going to join
Dad in Sister's office for a cup of tea.'

Later they went in together to see Darren who
was looking very pale and ill. They were allowed
only two minutes.

Davina leaned over to kiss him and he said in a
low voice,

'I'm sorry to cause you this trouble. It's cured me

of smoking anyway. I'm told I owe my life to my brother-in-law.'

His eyes sought Nick's, who replied soberly, 'You owe your life to Davina. She was putting your happiness before her own—that was why I arrived at the flat at the crucial moment. I was going to have a heart-to-heart talk with you. However, you must rest. That's the most important thing.'

Darren put out his hand to Davina, who kissed it, knowing that everything was going to be fine.

Darren and Cheryl were staying in the hospital overnight. John Tabor left for his appointment with his other son; Jocelyn and Davina went with Nick to the flat. The chair Darren, had sat in was a total wreck, but most of the damage had been done by smoke and the water from the firemen's hose.

By the time they left Davina was as grimy as Nick. As he drove back to his parents' home, Nick said, 'I think the most sensible thing to do is to make a clean break now with the shop and flat, my sweet. Cheryl and Darren can regard our home as theirs until we get them fixed up.'

She looked at him blankly. 'But what will Cheryl do?'

'Cheryl will fix herself up. She's wanted to take up nursing for a long time but didn't know how to tell you.'

'But what about Rex?'

'Rex is going around with a redhead at the moment. Cheryl never really loved him. You must know that, darling.'

'She did hint about it, but I understood her to be unsure of herself and her true feelings for Rex.'

Suddenly she was shining up at him and catching hold of his arm excitedly. There was laughter and relief in her voice. 'It might be the answer. Don't you see? Cheryl could be in the same hospital that Darren will eventually work in too after he qualifies. She could give him the incentive to do it.'

'You could be right.'

They arrived at the house to find that Nina had gone out. Her car was missing from the garage.

Nick said, 'What about us getting cleaned up and having a cold lunch! We'll forage it from the fridge. We could have it in our room since we're alone.'

Half an hour later, with Nick changed into slacks and silk shirt and Davina in a very pretty housecoat, they were bringing up food from the kitchen. Their room was filled with the delicious aroma of coffee as they ate cold chicken with green salad followed by cheese and crackers.

Davina looked at Nick, loving the newly washed fair hair drying into its usual tight curls, the well-cut mouth curving upwards at the corners endearingly, and the grey eyes mocking her sudden shyness. There was sheer bliss in the thought that this was only the first of many meals they would be sharing together as man and wife.

'Penny for your thoughts,' he offered lazily, refilling their coffee cups.

The words tumbled out. 'I was thinking what a waste it is for you to have such a head of delicious fair curls when they might have graced the head of some plain girl.'

His eyes twinkled wickedly. 'Maybe I can share them with our future daughters. I'm sure they'll be delighted to have such a gift from their dad. What do you think?'

Davina was beyond words. Her face was scarlet, but he only laughed.

'By the way, I think you should rest this afternoon,' he added. 'You've had enough excitement for one day.'

'What about you? Incidentally, you never said whether you passed out this morning during your gallant rescue.' Her green eyes misted. Her lips trembled. 'Thank you, darling, for saving my brother and sister. I love you very much, and I wish you would rest as well.'

'The idea had occurred to me,' he answered, smiling.

Nick went to close the curtains before giving her the warmth of his familiar grey gaze. Davina felt her heart leap in response and wondered however she could have been cold with him.

She rose to her feet and stood there feeling extremely foolish.

'I'm dreadfully sorry about last night,' she began.

He moved a provocative brow. 'How am I supposed to react to that? Slap your wrist and say that it mustn't happen again?' He surveyed her between narrowed lids. 'Come here,' he commanded.

Davina did not move. 'Stop teasing me,' she cried.

'I'm not teasing you,' Nick said calmly, and put out his arms.

She came to within arm's length of him to gaze at him with troubled eyes.

The words tumbled out. 'I've been such an idiot,' she admitted, near to tears.

'Aren't we all when we're in love, so stop making an issue of it. We've a lot of time to make up for.'

He took her into his arms and tenderly framed her face with his strong hands. He watched the frank enchantment of her face when she lifted her green eyes to his, and their gaze held fused by an aching need.

· Davina heard his breath rasp in his throat and a slow smile lifted the corners of his mouth to twinkle devilishly in his grey eyes.

Audaciously, he said, 'I take it that you have no objections to sharing a bed this afternoon, Mrs Tabor?'

'Absolutely none at all,' she breathed, trying to comprehend the utter joy washing over her so deliciously.

'Thanks.' The uneven timbre of his voice belied the laconic reply. 'We're all alone in the house.'

Slowly he unfastened the top buttons of her housecoat to push it down, caressing the outline of her shapeliness as he did so. His eyes darkened into an aching need and his arms tightened around her.

'No one to intrude upon our privacy,' he murmured, kissing her eyes and soft cheeks before moving down to her mouth.

This time there was no stiffening against him. Before the housecoat had fallen around her feet Davina had her arms tightly around his neck.

Every anguish, every pang, every doubt was purged away as joy so great that it became almost a pain held her heart in its grip.

The kiss went on and on until Davina pushed back enough to regain her lost breath.

Nick laughed unsteadily and kissed her hair. 'Was I too rough? I'm sorry.'

Her voice was low, almost incoherent. 'I liked it. Never stop loving me, Nick.'

Her lips moved against his firm brown throat as he bent to scoop her up into his arms.

'Do you realise, Mr Tabor, that it's after six o'clock and time to dress for dinner.'

Davina leaned over the recumbent figure of her husband stretched out contentedly beside her and kissed his nose.

He sighed and pulled her down to his lips. 'Don't nag, woman. I hate nagging women.'

'And I hate masterful, arrogant men ...'

'With blond hair?' His eyes twinkled with amusement. 'Well, you're stuck with one.'

She gurgled and kissed his throat. 'You heard me that day in the shop, didn't you, singing the praises of dark men? It was a kind of defence against you. You frightened me a little.'

'Nonsense. You were afraid of coming alive. Now you have I mean to keep you that way.'

'For ever,' she said dreamily.

'For ever,' he answered against her lips, and Davina knew that she would never want it any other way.

4 FREE

Harlequin Romances